BLACK
ROSE the

TIFFANY FORBES

The Black Rose

Copyright © 2019 by Tiffany Forbes.

This book is a work of fiction. Names, characters, businesses, organizations, places, events and incidents either are the product of the author's imagination or are used fictitiously. Any resemblance to actual persons, living or dead, events, or locales is entirely coincidental.

Book Creation & Design | Editor
DHBonner Virtual Solutions, LLC
www.dhbonner.net

ISBN: 978-0-578-54129-7

To those who have encouraged, inspired,
and believed in me, this is for you.
Thank you!

"The greatest tragedy in life is not death, but a life without a purpose." -Miles Munroe

PROLOGUE

Evelyn Rose woke up in the darkness, still tied to the steel pipe of the cold, moldy basement. She felt as if she were in a dark crypt as her breath came in short, loud rasps. At first, everything was a blur, and she had to blink several times to adjust her vision.

Where the hell *was* she? How was she going to get out? How long had she been here? How long... how long until...he came back?

Just as she started to calm herself, she heard foot-steps. They were slow. Steady. Loud. One step, then another. She waited and listened to what sounded like heavy boots pounding the pavement. They were getting closer.

A wave of panic washed over her.

She was shivering uncontrollably now, and not just from the clammy coldness of the basement. The tank top she was wearing was covered in blood, and so was her underwear. He had removed her clothes; she couldn't remember when.

Now, in the cold, she felt absolutely naked.

Looking around the room, she tried to make out a familiar presence, but there was none. She took in the thick stone walls, slick with moisture and mold. All that ran through her mind was that even if she tried to scream, no one would hear for miles. No one knew where she was. She was certain he had made sure of that.

He. Who was he?

Every part of her body lit up, and she suddenly became aware of the pain, especially the throbbing in the back of her head. Immediately, the memory flashed in her mind of him hitting her. She winced as she remembered trying to escape once, maybe two nights ago. She had almost been free, or so she had thought, but he had come out of nowhere and hit her with something hard. She distinctly remembered the floor rushing up to meet her and could only imagine how her body must have crumpled.

Jolting back to reality, she felt his menacing presence close to her now. Even in the hazy darkness, she felt his eyes—piercing, probing—and tried to look up, but couldn't. She felt vulnerable and didn't know what he was going to do to her this time, but from somewhere inside of her, a glimmer of determination flickered. This was not her day to die. This was not how it was going to happen.

She wasn't sure how long it had taken her — hours, maybe days? — But she had pulled and tugged at the ropes binding her hands and feet until they were becoming loose enough to get free. However, she needed to wait until the right time to make her move. She would wait until he came back.

And now, here he was, standing over her, and she barely made out something in his hand. Was it a knife? A gun? She tried again to look into his face, only to realize it was mostly covered by a hoodie.

"Please, let me go," she whispered.

She felt a tear running down her cheek and tried to protest some more, but he backed up into the middle of the room and turned on a single light bulb that was swinging from the ceiling. It wasn't bright, but it was blinding to her. She could see what was in his hands now; the blade of the knife was long and gleaming. She watched as he put it down on a small table, before walking back over to her.

"What do you want from me?" she asked.

In one sudden movement, he stepped closer to her and swung his hand, connecting with her right cheek. Then, she felt warm liquid began to flow down her lip. It was her blood. What was he going to do next? She had to think quickly. She made a conscious decision to fight like hell. She was not going to die here.

"Please, just let me go," she managed to whisper again.

The second blow to the jaw was worse than the first. Her head was spinning.

Silently, the man went back to the table in the middle of the room and picked up the knife. He knelt next to her and held the blade to her throat. She still couldn't see his face; he was blocking the light now. He raised the knife over her head.

"Please! My baby. Don't hurt my baby!"

Instantly, he stumbled backward, and dropped the knife. Then, after standing still for what seemed like forever, he slowly reached up and took off his hoodie.

She gasped as she immediately recognized him.

"No!" she screamed.

Quickly, almost instinctively, she swooped her right leg out, pinned the knife with her foot, pulling it toward her. Then, after unraveling the loosened ties, picked it up with her hand.

As the man leaped forward, she freed her hands and stabbed his leg. He dropped to his knees and groaned. She stabbed him in his torso.

He screamed.

She tried to get up, but her legs were wobbly, and her head was still spinning. She dropped to the floor again. She watched as the man winced and groaned in pain. She got to her knees and tried to crawl to the steps. He grabbed her ankle. She kicked him in the face as hard as she could, her bare heel connecting with his nose. He screamed again.

"You bitch!" he cried out. "I am going to kill you *and* your baby."

"There's no baby, you psycho!" She kicked him again.

The room joined her head and began to spin. Evelyn's breath became fast, and her heart raced faster and faster. She crawled over to the foot of the stairs and looked up at the top. The door was waiting for her. She had to get out, but she couldn't; she was too weak. Suddenly, the room seemed to stop moving, and there were two of everything...then three. She leaned against the railing of the stairs and stared at the man on the floor. He had stopped moving, stopped breathing, stopped crying.

Her husband was dead.

Everything went dark again.

BOOK I

CHAPTER 1

Ex-FBI PROFILER EVELYN ROSE DUBOIS COULD NOT stop smiling as she stepped into the departure lounge of JFK International airport. This was her first vacation in a long time, and she and her best friend Camille were on their way to the Caribbean for two weeks. She planned to spend most of it on the beach and in the warm sun with the blue sky and the clear blue water playing at her feet.

She needed this break. She needed a break, especially from Richard, her boss, with whom she had a complicated on and off relationship. Richard was getting too close, and she had to end things, and he wasn't happy with that. She didn't want a commitment right now, and it was partly due to a troubling past secret that she is carrying. But for now, she was going to the Virgin Islands to enjoy her fun in the sun with her best gal.

They found a seat not too far from the doorway that led to the entrance of the plane and plopped down in two empty seats. Getting from the checkpoint to the gate had been a long walk as her friend wanted to stop at every store and kiosk to look at magazines and books.

When they finally sat down, Camille noticed that her friend was staring off into the distance.

"Hey, where were you just now?" her friend asked, interrupting her thoughts.

"Just thinking about work." She lied. She couldn't have been thinking about work, because she had taken leave without pay a few months ago.

"Why are you thinking about work at a time like this? Why don't you think about doing something special for your birthday?" Camille asked, sipping on a diet coke she had bought from one of the many kiosks they had visited.

Evelyn laughed, "My birthday is not for two months."

"I know, but we can still plan something; we don't have to wait until then. You can invite some of your friends and—"

"You know I don't have friends, Camille; you're my only friend. And I hate celebrating my birthday. It just makes me feel older. The less I think about my age, the younger I feel."

"Hm, I just think you need to have some fun in your life Ev, all you do is go home and sit in front of the television or computer and sip wine. You need to get out more." her friend said.

"But I like staying home and drinking my wine."

"It's not healthy."

"Don't worry about me; I'll be fine. I'll make friends when I make them. As for now, work is my life, and I like it that way, okay? Plus, you and I taking a trip to the Islands is all the fun that I need right now." She smiled.

"Yea, the only reason why you're going on this trip is because I twisted your arm for the past four months."

Her friend reluctantly returned her smile.

They sat in the terminal of the airport in silence and waited until they heard their flight number called. Evelyn was excited and nervous at the same time. She hated flying, but she would do anything to get away from her life for two weeks, maybe even more.

Her cell phone buzzed in her handbag. "Shit!" she cursed under her breath. She looked over at her friend who was busy reading a magazine, before pulling out her phone and looking at the caller ID.

The number was blocked, so she put the phone back into her bag. She would turn it off, but she would wait until after they got on the plane.

"Would you ever kill for love?" Camille asked, still looking at the magazine.

"What?" Evelyn wondered why she would ask her something like that.

"I was watching this show on television last night... you know, those shows with the girls who will do anything for their men, even kill? So, I'm asking you if you met this guy and you fell totally over the moon in love with him, would you kill for love?"

Evelyn snickered, "I don't think so, would you?"

"Hmmm," Camille mused, looking back at her maga-zine. "Maybe."

"Are you serious?" Evelyn replied, wide-eyed, as she

turned towards this woman she thought she had known for well over ten years.

"Yea, I think I would," her friend said, grinning slyly while still looking at her magazine.

"Camille Melissa Somble, are you kidding me right now? You're sitting here, telling me if your husband asked you to do something illegal, you would do it because you love him?"

"Yep!" Camille said, before bursting out laughing.

"You are one sick woman, my friend." She said.

The gate attendant came over the loudspeaker and announced that the flight had arrived and that they would be boarding in about ten minutes.

Evelyn took her phone back out of her bag when she felt it begin to buzz again. She looked down at the caller ID and this time she saw that Richard was calling.

"What kind of game are you playing," she asked when she answered it.

"Evelyn, what are you talking about?" Richard said, seemingly surprised.

"You called me before from a blocked number to see if I would answer you. Look, Richard, I am going on vacation, and I don't need anything to stress me out right now, I need this to—"

"Wait, I never called you before. I just wanted to say have a safe flight, and we need to talk when you get back."

"Okay, we can talk when I get back, but I have to go now, my flight is about to board." Evelyn hung up the phone before Richard could say anything else. Just as she was putting the phone back into her bag, it buzzed again.

Blocked number… again.

Staring at the caller ID, she bit her lower lip, wondering if she should answer.

Evelyn was a bit paranoid and thought to herself that nothing good ever came from answering a blocked number. She found that out the hard way when she answered telemarketers and bill collectors. But then again, it was probably Richard messing with her.

Richard Elias, her ex, wanted a relationship, even talking about getting married one day, but she had to end that relationship. For her, he was moving too fast. Now he was her boss, and she had trouble maintaining a professional relationship with him, seeing that they already had sex and everything. She would never date her boss; that was a line she told herself she would never cross.

The attendant's voice came over the intercom again, notifying those in the waiting area that they were starting the boarding process, and proceeded to call the first numbers. She and Camille began to gather their stuff and walk towards the end of the line because they were booked in coach.

Her phone buzzed again in her bag. *Dammit! Are you kidding me?* she thought to herself as she glanced at the caller ID. Blocked number. This time she decided to answer it.

"Hello?" she said, trying to be calm.

There was no answer, but she could hear slow, steady breathing on the other end of the line.

"Who is this?" she whispered into the call so that no one around her could hear. "Please stop calling this number."

"No," the voice on the other end said, in a deep groggy voice before the call disconnected.

Evelyn froze and stared at the phone. It couldn't be. She was sure that she almost recognized the voice.

No.

"Ev, girl, our flight is here. Let's go," her best friend beckoned to her.

"Okay, okay. I'm coming," she said.

"Who was that?" Camille asked eyeing the phone in her left hand.

"I don't know. A wrong number, I guess," she said, putting her phone back into her bag.

Just as Evelyn looked up to answer her friend, she saw the man about 20-feet away. She didn't need glasses to tell that he was staring right at her. Suddenly, her heart started to race like it usually did whenever she was anxious, but it wasn't her nerves now. Her cheeks flushed, and she began to feel pale; the ground felt like it was going to swallow her up whole. He was just staring at her, and his smile was eerie, causing the hairs on the back of her neck to stand on end... and he had what looked like a phone to his ear.

"It can't be," she whispered to herself.

Her companion must have heard her because a confused Camille was looking at her now.

"Girl, you okay?" she asked.

Evelyn quickly turned to look back at the spot where the man had been standing. There was something about him that reminded her of the man who had been the love of her life; the man who had tortured her and left her almost for dead.

It was impossible, though; he was gone.

Glancing over at her best friend, who seemed deeply concerned about her, Evelyn shook it off.

"Yea, I'm fine," she said. "Let's go!"

CHAPTER 2

THE MEDIUM-BUILT MAN IN THE GREY BLAZER looked middle-aged, but was younger, and stood a few yards away from where Evelyn and Camille sat. He watched them as they walked over to the back of the line that led to the departure door. She was looking down at something, her phone maybe. He had a good vantage point of them from where he stood next to the male restroom; with a cup in one hand and a newspaper in the other, he had disguised himself as a potential tourist. He was sure that she would not suspect a thing. But why would she?

He had been following her for weeks and realized that she was smart and very aware of her surroundings.

Suddenly, as if Evelyn had sensed he was watching her, she looked up and turned in his direction. It was like a scene right out of a scary movie, but this wasn't a movie, it was reality. "Shit! had she spotted him?" He thought for a moment. No. he then realized that she was looking right past him. Relieved, he adjusted his glasses and took a sip from his cup. There was no way that she would recognize him; after all, he was wearing a disguise. He smiled to himself. She looked like she was worried about something, terrified maybe, he saw it on her face. He wondered if it was about that time to make the call again. No, he would wait until the plane landed in the Caribbean.

He wanted to make sure that he was among the last few people to board the airplane. He booked a first-class ticket and knew there was no way he would bump into them. He sipped on the coffee he purchased from the nearby Dunkin' Donuts again. It was hot just how he liked it.

As the line got shorter, he took up his duffle bag and slowly made his way to the line. He made sure that Evelyn and her friend were already on the plane before he boarded. He lifted his bag onto his shoulder, walked over to the airline hostess and gave her his ticket, smiled, nodded, and entered the aircraft. He made sure he packed light this time. Jeans, t-shirt, hat, sunglasses, and his camera were mostly what he needed to be incon-spicuous.

He took out his cell phone, punched in the number and typed, *'IM ON THE PLANE'* before turning it off and putting it into his jacket pocket. He was excited and nervous at the same time as he didn't like to fly, but he was glad he was sitting in first class where he could get alcohol and maybe sleep during most of the flight.

He walked down the aisle to the first-class cabin and

found his seat, 4B where an older woman was sitting in the seat next to the window. She looked nervous. He placed his duffle bag in the overhead compartment and sat down and placed his seat belt across his lap.

He took out a magazine from the seat pocket in front of him and began to scan the pages, but he wasn't reading. He was thinking about his trip and the things that he was going to do, and he smiled at this. He wondered what Evelyn and her friend were doing back in coach. He imagined the look on her face when he finally introduced himself. He couldn't wait to see that "Excuse me, sir," the lady sitting next to him said.

He was so deep into his own thoughts; he didn't notice her tapping him on his forearm.

Feeling a little annoyed, he plastered a fake smile on his face and turned in her direction.

"Yes, ma'am?" he asked her.

The woman looked slightly middle-aged, about 55 or 60 years old. Her red lipstick made her face look younger than she appeared to be, but the wrinkles around her eyes could not hide.

She leaned into him and spoke a little softer now.

"I'm so sorry to bother you, Dear, but do you mind if we switch seats? I really don't feel comfortable sitting next to the window. I sort of have a fear of heights." "Sure," the man said and got up to give her his seat.

They exchanged seats and sat down and put on their seat belts, the young flight attendant walked past them and checked to see if everyone had put their seat belt. Then the captain came over the intercom and told everyone that the flight was ready for takeoff. The man wasn't sure if the lady beside him heard anything that he said, because when she sat down, she didn't stop yapping. He wondered if she would ever stop talking.

He looked over at the old woman a couple of times and smiled at her, pretending to listen to her consistent yapping. He didn't want to be rude and tell her to shut up because she seemed so nice, but he was suddenly getting a headache. He closed his eyes for a minute, hoping that she would get the drift, but the woman was going on and on about God's knows what.

A middle-aged woman appeared in the aisle and started to demonstrate the safety procedures for the flight, and suddenly, the old woman did shut up. He let out a sigh of relief. He listened to the flight attendant for a few minutes; then his mind trailed off.

Evelyn. Sweet Evelyn, what would he do when he came face to face with her? Would he be able to do what he had planned, or would he be overcome by her beauty? He had to admit she was beautiful, but he had to focus, he had to stick to the plan. Maybe he would make it look like an accident. He grinned.

After all, accidents do happen.

CHAPTER 3

*"Sometimes we don't even realize how much
this world is full of insane, messed up people until we
come in contact with one of them."*

EVELYN THOUGHT ABOUT THAT AS SHE LOOKED OUT
the airplane window. They had been flying for only two
and a half hours already, and the captain said that they
would soon take their final descent into St. Thomas. She
looked across at her best friend who was asleep for most
of the plane ride.

She had awoken when the flight attendant was
serving snacks then quickly fell asleep again. Before
falling into a deep sleep, Camille had asked her about
why she looked so worried back at the airport, and who
was on the phone? Evelyn was happy when she finally
gave up asking and nodded away. She didn't bother to
wake her. She was glad she didn't have to talk about it.

She had kept nothing from her best friend before, but this was one thing she couldn't let her in on, at least not yet.

She was on vacation, and all she wanted to do was lay on the beach and soak up some sun and enjoy the moment.

She closed her eyes and leaned back into the seat, and there he was again, standing across the airport and staring at her. She had to pretend to look past him at something else as to not give away that she was really looking at him. She knew she had seen him before, following her, but she couldn't be certain. She was very alert about her surroundings, which was an important thing that she learned from working in the FBI and also from her past life, so she was definite she had seen him before. But why would he be following her? Who was he?

Then a creepy grin crept across his lips. The image made her shudder, and she opened her eyes again.

Why couldn't she get that image out of her head? She knew there was no way that could have been him. Closing her eyes now was out of the question.

Evelyn glanced over at her friend who stirred in her seat; Cam's eyes fluttered open, she looked around to orient herself, and then leaned forward to straighten her seat. "Are we there yet?" she asked.

"You watch too much TV," Evelyn said.

Camille chuckled.

"Not yet, we are about 20 minutes or so away. Evelyn answered.

"Did you even get to sleep Ev?"

She was about to tell her she couldn't sleep because

of what she saw back at the airport, but all she said was, "A little," then shrugged.

The plane landed in the U.S. Virgin Islands at about 2:28 pm. The weather was nice and warm in the summer there and not like the oppressive heat they had just come from in New York. She was happy to be anywhere at this moment. She just had to get away from the chaos and complication that was her life. Even if it was for just a little while, she would feel liberated.

She looked around at the scenery, it was nice. The air was clean, and she could even smell the ocean. She took a deep breath and looked around for Camille who had turned on the phone from the time they landed. She was telling her husband she had arrived and asked about her girls.

Evelyn wasn't jealous since she never wanted kids. She had almost fallen into that trap once, but that was another lifetime.

Doing a little jog to catch up with Evelyn as they walked through the terminal to find the baggage claim, Camille exclaimed, "Isn't this exciting?"

"I know, right? This place is amazing!" she responded, returning her friend's excitement.

The airport was small in comparison to what they were used to, so they quickly found the baggage claim area and waited for their luggage. Ten minutes later, they had grabbed their bags and headed to a waiting taxi that took them to their hotel.

They sat back and enjoyed the scenery; they had never been to an island in the Caribbean before. Evelyn had traveled to different countries for work, but no other place came close to even looking like this. She never saw water so blue in all her life; you could practically see right to the bottom. She had forgotten all about the scene at the airport, and Richard as she couldn't stop beaming at the sight.

Camille was busy asking the taxi man loads of questions about the place.

"Have you been here before?" the taxi man then turned to Evelyn and asked when they arrived at the traffic lights.

"No, I haven't, but it is beautiful." She said.

"How long do you guys plan on staying here?" he asked.

"About two weeks," they said in unison, and then both laughed.

He handed them his business card. "If you ever need a taxi to tour the island or anything, just give me a call. My name is Kevin."

"It's nice to meet you, Kevin," Camille said. We definitely will give you a call."

Without hesitating, Camille took the card, read it, and then showed it to Evelyn who was looking out the window.

"Girl, are you ok? Where are you right now?" Camille asked.

"I'm good; I'm just taking it all in. I wish we could stay here forever."

"And leave my husband and kids back home? I don't think so."

"Well, maybe you can't, but I can. I don't have nobody to stop me or hold me down."

"What about Richard? You know he still cares about you, right?" Camille asked.

Evelyn nodded and gazed back out of the window. She wondered what it would be like to live in a place like this. For now, she was going to enjoy this trip. For now, she would take it all in. For now, she was happy.

Of course, she had no idea that the guy from the airport was sitting in the taxi right behind them.

CHAPTER 4

THEY FINALLY ARRIVED AT LINDBERG BAY RESORT, where they checked in and got the keys to their suite. Evelyn and Camille unpacked their suitcases and settled into their room. They had booked a suite with two double beds, a mini-kitchen, a TV area, and a huge bathroom, but this room was beyond anything that she had expected. The room was immaculately clean, and they had a perfect view of the ocean.

Evelyn turned her phone on and looked at it. Five missed calls; one from her mom with whom she hadn't spoken in a while and the four others from Richard. She decided that she would call her mom later, and she didn't want to hear from Richard, since he had been so clingy lately, which was a quality she hated most in men. She was the girl who just wanted a man for the physical, no strings attached.

As she put the phone on the table and plugged in the charger, the phone buzzed. The caller ID read "Richard."

She cursed under her breath. Camille, who was sitting on the other bed looked up at her.

"Who was that?" She asked.

"Richard. He keeps calling I guess to see if we arrived safely. He's tiptoeing on my last nerve."

"Oh, I didn't know that you two were back together again."

"We are not back together, but he will not stop calling," she told her friend.

"Maybe he just wants to make sure that everything is ok. He is such a great guy; I think you should give him a second chance."

"Yea, well... he lost that privilege when he became my boss. You know I don't like to be controlled. Plus, I can't take this clinginess." Evelyn said.

"What exactly is it you want, Evelyn?" her friend asked her.

"I want great, mind-blowing sex!"

They both laughed.

"So, I don't think you ever talked about what happened at the airport," Camille prodded, gently.

"What do you mean?" Evelyn asked, pretending not to know what her friend was asking her.

"Don't do that. You know what I mean. You were staring at the phone like something was wrong with it, and when you looked up, your face almost turned white. I know when there is something wrong, Evelyn Rose. So, what's been going on with you lately?"

She finally opened up and told her friend the truth.

After all, she knew that she was the only one she could count on.

She sighed, "I think I'm being followed, and I thought I saw the person at the airport. But I guess I'm just being paranoid."

"Is that all? Girl, I thought someone had died, trust me, you are tired and just need to put that brain of yours to rest. Look where we are right now. I suggest we both relax, have a lot of fun, and try to forget about everything. Hey, whoever it is, they won't find you here."

Evelyn felt a little better now that her friend had reassured her, but she would not let her guard down.

"Girl, I'm starving! What are we getting for dinner?" Camille asked, trying to break the mood.

"I need a drink myself," Evelyn responded in agreement. So, they both showered, got dressed, and headed downstairs to the bar they had passed on the way up to the room.

Later in the evening, after they had eaten dinner, Evelyn stayed at the bar while Camille went back upstairs to the room to call her husband. She was far from tired, so she sat and drank a few beers and talked to a few people who told her about the Island.

"You should take the ferry and visit some of the other neighboring Islands while you're here," the bartender suggested.

Another guy shouted from across the bar. "You'd love it." as he winked and cheered her with a bottle of beer.

Intrigued as much by the comment as the striking attractiveness of the man, she ignored her inhibitions, got up from her stool and walked over to the end of the bar where the man sat.

"Hi, I'm Evelyn," She said, introducing herself. He had an easy charm to him, and she could feel an attraction growing, and immediately she liked what she saw. She noticed that he wasn't wearing a wedding ring, but she sensed that he was hiding something; he seemed guarded somehow, but she decided to take a shot anyway, it couldn't hurt.

"Are you from here?" Evelyn asked the man.

"Nope, I'm a tourist just like you." He smiled.

"So, Mr. Tourist, are you married?" she asked him, in a half-joking fashion.

"You just get right into it huh?" he asked as he seemed to blush a little.

Evelyn didn't like to play games, she got right to the point; and a few drinks later they eventually found a quiet place outside the hotel and sat and talked for a while.

"You are very beautiful," the man said gazing into her eyes. "How is it that a woman like you haven't been snatched already?"

"Maybe I haven't found the right snatcher," she replied.

He smoothed her face with his hands and rested on her chin before he pulled her into him and gave her a kiss on her lips. His lips were smooth and tender to the touch. It was the perfect kiss. They lingered there for five seconds before he let go. She counted.

Damn, what was it about him that was so irresistible?

So safe? She snapped out of her thoughts when she heard him.

"You want to go for a walk?" he asked while standing. He took her hand in his and lead the way. They walked along the poolside of the hotel, then past the restaurant and then toward a little area where restrooms were.

They had passed a dark walkway probably used as a service entrance to deliver goods to the restaurant when Evelyn felt a tug on her arm, and she was being pulled backward into the darkness.

Then she realized what was happening.

The man wasn't so nice after all. He was just like all the other men out there that she met; he wanted something, and whatever he was after, he would not get it. The man stood behind her with his hand wrapped around her neck, but he was sure not to squeeze tight; it was just enough to get her to submit to him.

"What do you want?" she whispered. "You want money? I can give you money, just let go of me, please." She begged. Evelyn thought that if she remained calm and not fight back that he would not hurt her. She stayed aware of him because although she was never in this situation before, she was trained for this.

She faked a little cry, "Please, don't hurt me I can give you whatever you want, just let me go."

The man laughed a little and licked her face and that's when Evelyn snapped. She eased into her shoulder side bag slowly while the man held on tighter to her and with one quick movement, she slashed his hand with a pocket knife she always carried with her.

"You Bitch!" he screamed and loosened his grip.

She then turned around and kicked him in his groin and he wailed as he fell to the ground on his knees. This felt like déjà vu. Only the last time, the man had died.

No. she wouldn't kill him, but she would leave a lasting impression in his memory. She watched as the man winced and groaned in pain. She kneeled next to him and reached into his pants pocket and pulled out his ID. At least he was who he said he was, but another thing she saw was a picture of him and some woman and his wedding band hiding in his wallet.

"Well, lookie here. Aren't we the handsome liar? Mr. tourist has a wife. I wonder what wifey would say if she found out what you were doing tonight." She said playfully, waving the photo back and forth in his face.

"Please, don't. I'm sorry," he begged.

"Please, don't," she mocked. "Mr. tourist is not such a tough guy now, is he? You make me sick." She said and kicked him in his stomach, and he groaned again.

She stood over him and peered at him, she was angry, but she felt a little sorry for him simultaneously. This situation took her down memory lane. But she was prepared this time. Or so she thought, because when she looked up she locked eyes with him, the man she saw at the airport. And as if the flood gates had suddenly unlocked her memory, it was all coming back to her. She had seen him before, on several different occasions. Was he really following her? Her imagination was not playing tricks on her this time as she had previously thought. She gasped. Her heart raced and her knees felt like jelly. She just stood and stared.

"What the—", was all that she would mutter.

The man smiled, that awful creepy smile and turned and disappeared in the darkness.

She wanted to run and catch up to him, but when she turned the corner, he was nowhere to be found. Was she seeing things again?

She left the man on the ground wailing in pain and hurried back up to the room as if nothing had happened.

Little did she know that her nightmares were just starting.

CHAPTER 5

By the time Evelyn got back to the hotel room, Camille was in a deep sleep and there was no sense in trying to wake her. Instead of turning on the light to the room she only turned on the lamp that was next to her bed. Evelyn didn't bother to take a shower as she was feeling a bit exhausted and she figured that it was maybe from jetlag or she was buzzed from the six or seven beers that she drank earlier; she couldn't remember how many. She reached into the suitcase and pulled out her pajamas, change into them and crawled under the covers. She wasn't drunk but it was enough to give her a slight headache. As she was about to turn off the lamp, she noticed her cell phone light blinking on the charger.

"Oh, crap," she whispered.

She had forgotten to make a call to tell her mom that had arrived safe and that she shouldn't worry about her. But when she took the phone from the charger, she noticed that it was a text message, not from her mother but from Richard.

Please call me, we need to talk
I'm really worried about you

She ignored it and turned on her side to face the window, but she could not sleep that night; she tossed and turned as visions of her past mixed with events of that night, entered her mind. She saw his face again. The man at the airport, then she saw her ex-husband, it was like somehow the two faces had warped into one. It was something out of a horror movie.

Hardly anyone knew about her ex-husband. She met him when she decided to run away from home to get away from everything that was causing her emotional pain. She tried to run from her past. That was when she met Ronald at the lowest point in her life. He was so charming and sweet at first.

They had only dated a few months before they got married. She didn't tell anyone, not even her parents. Her mom was sick with minor heart trouble and her father had left them when she was young. But her parents had an off-again and on-again relationship before he left, and they fought constantly and the only good thing about her father leaving was that he left her with a lump sum of money. She guessed that was part of his guilt, so she was able to leave her life and her job and move to another country, Canada.

Canada is where she met Ronald Gregory Dubois.

The most handsome, intelligent man she had ever met; and his accent drove her crazy. She later learned that his family came to Canada from Trinidad. He was five years younger than her, but she didn't care about age. He was everything that she thought she needed.

Evelyn and Ronald got married at the courthouse, a small and intimate affair. With only the two of them, Ron's brother Eric, and her cousin Tiana with whom she briefly lived when she moved to Canada. Tiana was a Christian and very active in the church; so, she was pleased when Evelyn and Ronald decided to get married before they had sex, she even encouraged their marriage.

At first sight, Ronald and Evelyn were inseparable and they didn't hide their love for one another, not even in the public eye. But that was on the outside. Evelyn found out a year into the marriage who Ronald really was.

The first time he hit her, it took Evelyn by surprise. She was in such shock that she didn't know what to do at first. She just stood there in the kitchen, staring at him as he walked nonchalantly into the living room and sat on the sofa. She had always told herself that no one, especially a man, would put his hands on her. But this one caught her off guard. She thought their relationship was good, so how did it come to this? She went into the living room to confront him and stood over him while he lay on the couch with his eyes closed.

Was he drunk? No.

Ronald looked at her with one eye open and the other closed then he closed it again.

"What?" he said seemingly aggravated.

"You just hit me and now you're asking me what. What did I do to deserve you putting your hands on me?"

"Don't be so dramatic. I barely touched you."

"Are you freaking kidding me?" she was yelling now.

Ron got up from the chair now and faced her. "Look I'm sorry, I got carried away; it won't happen again so stop nagging me." Then he turned and headed down the hall to their room and slammed the door.

But it did happen again. As a matter of fact, it happened several times after that day. He had broken her arm, cracked a rib, and blackened her eye. He even threatened that if she ever left him, he would kill her. Her own husband who she adored, whom she loved from the first time that she laid eyes on him. She tried to fight back a few times, but it only made matters worse.

Evelyn secretly decided to join a self-defense class or a boxing class, anything to defend herself from the monster that she had mysteriously created. At the time she had no one to run to. She had to learn to fight on her own or die. The latter was out of the question.

While her husband was at work or out of the country she would train, run five miles, five days per week. When she was home, she tried to stay on his good side, at least until she felt she was strong enough to fight back. But nothing seemed perfect to him. He would start arguing about every little thing and her walking away made things worse. She wanted to give up, to give in to the beatings. No. she wasn't going to do that.

Two months later she decided that it was time for her

to move on, to move back home to her familiar surroundings. So that's when she decided to pack her bags one day while he was at work and move back in with her cousin. But he found her. He begged and pleaded for her to come back, and she did. She believed his lies when he cried in front of her and said he was sorry and that he would go to therapy if she would come back home. But that was short lived; the fights and the beatings continued. For months after that, she walked around like a zombie, immune to the hurt and the pain and the disrespect. The only thing left to do was to go back home. And when she did, she would never look back.

She saw his face now; he was coming towards her with the knife. He was smiling. It was like that eerie smile of the guy that she saw earlier, at the airport, downstairs at the hotel bar. Who was he? Why was he here? Was she imagining all this? Had her dead husband come back to take revenge in some way, somehow?

Impossible.

Maybe he had mistaken her for someone else, maybe he was here on vacation also. Too many maybes. "Get it together Evelyn, you're being paranoid again," she said, softly scolding herself.

Enough.

She needed to get some sleep. She sat up in bed and dug into the side table and took out a aspirin and swallowed it down with some water she got from the bathroom tap. There was no way that she was going to get any sleep now. She turned and twisted and listened to her best friend snore softly in the other bed across from her.

Minutes passed, maybe hours, and Evelyn was still struggling to get some sleep. The room was dark except for the light that illuminated from the outside through the window. Evelyn blinked several times as she noticed a dark silhouette covering most of the windows. How was this possible when they were several floors up? The figure looked like they were peering into the window right at her, but she could not make out a face.

Who was that?

She eased over to the side of the bed, making sure not to take her eyes away from the window. She slid out of bed slowly making her way to the window. Halfway there, the face became clearer, and she now recognized him. The figure. She was staring into his eyes. Her husband's eyes; her dead husband's eyes. "Ronald?" she whispered.

Then she was awake.

CHAPTER 6

EARLY THE NEXT MORNING, WHEN EVELYN GOT UP, she didn't see Camille, but she wasn't worried about her friend. Cam was tough, and she could handle herself; probably better than Evelyn had done last night. She remembered it as clear as day, despite her efforts to forget. She'd only had a few drinks, at least six or seven, but she still hadn't gotten drunk. As a matter of fact, she had never gotten drunk in her life, but that didn't stop her head from feeling like it was about to split wide open.

She slipped on her robe and slippers and walked past the coffee table when she saw the note from Camille. 'Went for a run, will be back in an hour.' She wondered what time she left and thought it must have been very early. She took a shower and let the steam slowly engulf her body. After her long shower, she sat in her robe and decided to call Richard. The call went directly to voice mail. "Great," she muttered to herself. The next call was to her mom. Although she and her mom were once very close, they had become a little distant after the incident, but she checked in on her every now and again so that she wouldn't worry about her. The call was brief because her mother had to run some errands and promised to call her back later that day. No pleasantries needed. She seldom said I love you to anyone; it was weird. Evelyn wondered why that was.

She went to the table and poured herself some coffee. Taking a sip, she thought about her childhood, how her mother would always be there for her. She remembered the days when she heard her mother crying in her room after her father had left them. "We will always be together, my sweet baby girl." She knew it was a lie because he had and moved to another country. She never heard from him again, apart from occasional gifts and birthday cards that didn't mean anything to her.

That was maybe why most of her relationships didn't last. Maybe that was why she didn't want to commit. She had heard those words one morning when she sat in the therapist office after her near-fatal accident. An accident that she made sure to happen. It had happened years ago. The day that she met Camille, and Camille had saved her life. At that point, she felt like she was in a whirlwind spiraling out of control. The only thing left to do... was take her own life.

Her phone buzzed in her hand and took her out of her thoughts. Richard. After a momentary hesitation, she answered the phone. Richard immediately started scolding her about how much he worried about her and her safety, but that didn't faze Evelyn.

"We need to talk," he told her.

"Talk," she replied and sighed. She wasn't in the mood right now for an argument, especially not from Richard. It was exhausting talking to him sometimes, but she listened intently.

"Are you finished?" she asked him when she got tired of him talking. "There are some things I have to go and do today."

"When can I call you again?"

"I'm not really in the mood to talk about anything, and as a matter of fact, we have nothing more to talk about. I'm on vacation, and just in case you forgot, we are no longer in a relationship." Evelyn closed her eyes and sighed. "Look, Richard. I'm not trying to be rude, but I am very capable of taking care of myself, you don't need to keep checking up on me."

"So that's it?" he asked her.

She thought about that for a moment, "Yes, I think it's best that we take a break for a while. I will call you when I get back home, ok?" she said, then hung up the phone.

Ten minutes later, Camille came into the room and saw Evelyn sitting on the side of the bed dressed in a white t-shirt and jeans shorts, looking into her beach bag.

"Look who's ready for the beach," her friend laughed.

"Yea, you better hurry up or I will leave you behind. Plus, I'm starving; we need to get some breakfast before we head out."

"Sure, let me just take a quick shower then we are out of here."

Camille grabbed a change of clothes from her suitcase. She was about to pass by Evelyn when she stopped and saw something near the foot of the bed on the floor. She picked it up and showed it to Evelyn. "Who's this wallet for Ev?" She calmly asked.

Evelyn froze, she had to think quickly; if she tried to lie about it, her friend would catch on. She gave it a try anyway.

"Oh, I found it on my way to the room last night, some drunk guy must have dropped it. I thought I would leave it at the front desk this morning when we go out." She swallowed hard and continued looking into her bag as to not give herself away.

Camille shrugged and tossed the wallet on the bed without giving it a second thought.

"By the way," she started again. "Girl, did you have a nightmare? You were talking in your sleep all night," she said.

Evelyn shrugged, and without another word, Camille disappeared into the bathroom. Soon after, Evelyn heard the shower running. She took the wallet from the bed and put it into the drawer of the bedside table under some magazines. She wouldn't get the wallet back to him today; she was going to teach him a lesson. In the meantime, her thoughts went back to the guy that was looking at her. Had he seen what happened? She was sure of it. Why hadn't he stopped her? Had he gone to the police or the hotel security?

No, he wanted something. She thought about that for a moment. It was not a coincidence that the man was at the airport, now last night he was only a few yards away standing and watching her while she was with her attacker.

She had never really told her best friend about her ex; about being shot and stabbed and left for dead. Not even her mom knew. She was good at keeping secrets, and that was the best kept one yet. How was she to tell the people who loved and trusted her that she had committed a crime, and that she had to do it in self-defense? How could she tell her family that she had almost died? It wouldn't be fair to them. She wished she could just lock it in a safe and throw away the key forever.

Camille emerged from the bathroom, fully dressed in a short white sundress and lip gloss and light makeup.

"Excuse me," Evelyn cleared her throat, "We are going to the beach, not the club. Why are you so dressed up?"

"Don't worry. I have my bathing suit and a change of clothes in the bag," she replied. "But I need to call my husband before we leave; I want to see how the girls are doing. And send him a little sexy selfie," she added, chuckling.

"Well, hurry up ma'am," Evelyn said.

"I'll make the call while we're at breakfast."

"Good!" Evelyn said and grabbed her bag.

When they got to the door and opened it, Evelyn stood frozen in the doorway and stared down at her feet when Camille came up behind her.

"What are you looking at? Ev?" she asked.

She went closer to the friend and followed her gaze, and that's when she saw it.

"What the hell is that," Camille asked her.

Right there in front of the door, they saw a single rose with a red ribbon wrapped around it.

A black rose.

CHAPTER 7

THE MAN SAT AS LOW AS HE POSSIBLY COULD IN THE backseat of the taxi bus as to not give away his presence. He quietly listened to the taxi driver, and the women go back and forth about their visits to the island. He didn't need to get any luggage as he was already carrying it with him on the plane. That made it easy for him to watch them from afar, watch them request a taxi and slip in before they even notice him. He was seemingly good at being invisible.

For most of the drive, the women were quiet. He noticed Evelyn staring out of the bus window, not acknowledging the driver or her best friend as they go on and on about the island, the sites, the best places to eat and hang out and so on.

He had been watching Evelyn for weeks. He followed her wherever she went and became familiar with the things she liked, her favorite foods, the gym she frequented, supermarket, work. He slipped into her apartment one night when she went out with her girl-friend for dinner. He broke into her computer and cloned it so that he was able to see what she was doing when he wasn't there. That was how he was able to see when and where she was going on vacation, and which hotel they were going to stay in.

She had almost caught him that very same night.

She came home early from dinner, and he wasn't sure why, which caused him to have to slip under her bed quickly. He waited until she was dead asleep then he snuck out. That was a close call.

Now, he was in a hotel room not too far from the ladies. He made sure to stay close so that he would see when they entered and exited their room; they had no choice but to pass by his room on the way out.

He took out his cell phone and placed the call to his employer—the man who had hired him to follow Evelyn and Camille to the Caribbean.

"I'm at the hotel now." He said to the man on the other end of the call.

"Good, did they see you?" the employer asked.

"No, I don't think so, but I thought she might have noticed me for a second at the airport." He said.

"What?" his employer yelled.

"Don't worry about it; she didn't see me."

"Ok," there was a brief pause on the line, then the man heard clicking on the other end of the phone. "I need you to do me a favor." He said.

"Yea, what's that?" the man asked.

"Don't do anything until I tell you to. Just sit tight and

keep your distance, I don't want any of them suspecting you. These women are very smart, and they will figure it out if anything is out of the ordinary."

"I hear you; I got this all under control," the man said.

"I know you hear me, but do you understand?" his employer asked.

"Yes, Sir," he said mockingly, like he was in the army saluting his sergeant.

"Did you send the rose?"

"Yup, one single rose just like you requested." The man said, smiling to himself. If only he could have seen the look on Evelyn's face when she saw the black rose waiting for her by her hotel room door. It must have been priceless.

"Good, just make sure that she doesn't get herself into any trouble; the last thing I want is an international tragedy on my hands. I can just see it now, 'Ex-profiler for the FBI found dead in the Caribbean,' that's the last thing I want to see in the headlines."

"I know why you paid me; you don't have to keep pounding it into my brain like I'm a child."

"Fine," his employer said, then the phone disconnected.

The conversation between the two men was short, just like he liked it. "Don't do anything until I tell you... sit tight..." the words played over and over in his head, and that made him angry, "who the hell does he think he is anyway?" he grumbled to himself.

The man unpacked his duffle bag and sat on the side of the bed. It was time to go through his plans exactly. He was also good at what he did. After all, he had been following Ms. Evelyn for weeks now, and she had no idea. No one had any idea, not even his employer. He had been following her even before he got the job.

He had to think.

What would be the best way to get rid of her body, their bodies? An accident or a murder? A murder would send a better message, to his employer, especially. He didn't like the guy one bit.

"Keep your cool man," the guy said to himself. He got up and paced the room for several minutes then he stopped. He wasn't thinking clearly; he needed a drink or maybe two. Then he would go back to planning.

There was only one mission in mind when he left the terminal of the Cyril King International Airport — and now he had to decide which one of the two women he was going to kill first.

CHAPTER 8

THE DAY WAS BRIGHT AND SUNNY WHEN EVELYN AND Camille left the hotel in a taxi and headed to the ferry to visit the other island the man at the bar had told her about. They had researched it while they were at breakfast and from the pictures on the internet, the man was right about the beaches being so pristine; she had never seen water so blue in all her life.

Tortola. The largest of the British Virgin Islands was like a whole other country. Natures little secret they had called it. And Evelyn wondered why that was. It didn't matter because she was in paradise.

When they landed and got off of the ferry, they were told that the last ferry back to St. Thomas was at 5:00 pm.

They took a taxi which took them to a nearby beach and where they settled into a couple of the beach chairs that were empty. It was cool and breezy, which made

Evelyn wish that she could stay there for the rest of her life.

There were a few people around, some local and others that looked like tourists, then Camille noticed a group of people cooking and dancing at the other end of the beach where it looked like a party was going on; there was music and laughing and talking.

"I wonder what's going on over there," Camille said, "It looks like a party."

"You want us to go and see?" Evelyn said, easing out of her beach chair.

"I don't think so, missy. I'm not into crashing parties today."

"It will be fun, let's just go and take a look then come right back."

"I thought we were here to relax for a bit?"

"Having fun is part of relaxation, girl, come on and stop acting shy."

Against Camille's protests, Evelyn got up, dragging Camille with her, and they slowly walked over to the party to see what was going on.

"I can't believe you're dragging me to this thing against my will, what kind of friend are you anyway?" Camille said.

Evelyn hooked her hand in her friend's, "I'm a very good friend, and so are you, and that is why we are here today, to relax and have some fun. And if it wasn't for you, my very best friend, I wouldn't be living today."

"You trying to make me cry? Or is this your way of working your reverse psychology on me?" Camille asked.

"A little bit of both," Evelyn chuckled. "Now let's go and have some fun on this beach girl."

The truth was, Camille was up for whatever Evelyn wanted to do on this trip; she had her girl's back now just like she had her back when they first met. Meeting Evelyn that night was like it was destined for them to be friends and Camille took that role very seriously. She knew that Evelyn was a free spirit, but she was also tough and had the ability to fend for herself. She was the type of person that did whatever she wanted and dealt with the consequences later. But she was also a grown woman and Camille was not going to be that person to tell her friend what she could or could not do, but it was still her job to keep her best friend out of trouble, and that's why she was there.

With every step, the people and the party got closer and closer. Evelyn was giddy, but Camille swallowed hard. She was a bit nervous as she didn't know these people and she didn't know what they were going to get into. But from the dancer's faces, it looked like they were having fun. The music grew louder and louder as they got closer, and before they knew it, they were in the middle of the scene.

Evelyn started swaying to the music while Camille held on to her a little tighter. "Girl, if you don't relax, I won't have any circulation left in my arm."

Evelyn loosened her friend's grip and twirled her around in the sand and began moving to the music. They both started laughing. The people standing nearby looking on were also swaying, and now everybody at the party was dancing. This is what Evelyn needed, to let loose and have a good time. She didn't even think about the man at the airport or even Richard. This was the happiest that Evelyn had been in a long time.

"I like your moves."

Evelyn jumped as she turned and saw a dark and handsome man standing behind her, holding three bottles of beer.

"Excuse me?" she replied.

"I was saying that I liked your moves," he repeated again, handing her one of the beers and the other to Camille.

"Thanks," she said, And I like your accent, she wanted to say, but she smiled at him instead.

"Y'all want something to eat?" he asked.

"No, we're fine," Camille spoke up before Evelyn had a chance to say anything.

Evelyn turned and gave her friend a nudge and turned back and smiled at the man again.

"Sure." She said.

The man nodded them over with his head for them to follow him to an area of the beach where they had a pot on an open fire. Evelyn only saw this on television when she used to watch those camping shows. She was intrigued and wanted to know what was cooking in the big cast iron pot.

"Wow, I hope they're not cooking a body in there," she said to the man then leaned over to her friend, "I've never seen a pot that big," Evelyn whispered to her friend.

"Girl, stop it," Camille said, poking her with her elbow.

The man lifted the pot's lid, and the most amazing aroma filled the atmosphere, and Evelyn closed her eyes and inhaled it for just a moment.

"Man, that smells amazing, what is it?" Camille said

"Don't worry, it's not a body," the man winked at her, taking two disposable plates from a nearby bag hanging on a tree branch and proceeding to fill them with food. He gave one to Evelyn and the other to Camille who reluctantly looked at it.

"It does smell amazing," Evelyn said, and she took her fork and searched the food to see what was inside. After one bite of the food, Evelyn thought that she was in heaven. "I would like to meet the person who cooked this wonderful meal," she said.

"Hi, my name is Anthony St. Patrick, and it is nice to meet such beautiful women as you two," He said.

"Wait, you cooked this?" Evelyn asked in disbelief. Wide-eyed, she waited for him to say 'no, I'm just joking,' but he didn't. He simply continued to watch her and smile, which made Evelyn blush a little bit.

"So, what's your name beautiful?" he asked.

"I'm Evelyn, and this is my best friend, Camille."

Camille was busy looking in the direction of the other people and slowly trying to keep her movements in beat with the music while Evelyn and Anthony chatted and ate. This was the first time in a long time that she had seen Evelyn smile like she did today.

They didn't realize how long they had been there

until Camille quickly glanced at her watch and noticed that if they didn't get moving now, they would miss the last boat leaving to head back to the Hotel.

By this time, Evelyn and Anthony were walking slowly down near the water; Camille waved to her, but she didn't seem to notice. Camille then got both of their bags and caught up to Evelyn and grabbed her by the arm in order to get her attention.

"I'm sorry, but if we don't leave now, we are going to miss the boat back to St. Thomas."

"So? Can't you see I'm having a good time, maybe we should stay over."

"Girl, are you crazy? And sleep where? This is not a camping trip; let's go." She then leaned in and whispered to Evelyn, "We don't know these people. Come on."

"We can find a hotel tonight, I'm pretty sure there's a lot of hotels around, we are sure to find a vacant room in one of them," Evelyn said.

"Okay, fine. But first thing tomorrow morning we are catching the first ferry that leaves this island, you understand me?" Camille said.

Evelyn kissed her friend on the cheek and went back over to talk to Anthony. Evelyn decided that she and Camille would spend the weekend on the Island so that she can get to know Anthony a little better. Camille didn't feel right about it but decided that she wasn't going to leave her friend in case anything happened while she was gone.

CHAPTER 9

THAT NIGHT, EVELYN AND CAMILLE STAYED AT A cheap hotel, only a five-minute drive from the dock. Anthony called ahead and made a reservation for the ladies. It wasn't the best place, but at least they had somewhere to stay, and it would only be one night. Anthony and Evelyn stayed downstairs for a while in the bar and talked some more, while Camille left them and went to the room. "I will be up shortly," Evelyn had said, but shortly had turned into hours.

By the time Evelyn got upstairs with Camille, she was beaming, and Camille was steaming, she noticed that she was pacing the room and talking to herself. She didn't even notice that Evelyn had entered the room, and Evelyn couldn't make out what she was saying. When Evelyn closed the door shut, Camille jumped.

"What the—" she stopped when she saw it was Evelyn.

"What the hell are you doing, who are you talking to?" Evelyn asked.

"I thought you said you would be right up, what took you so long? Do you enjoy making me worry about you?"

"Girl, I'm sorry, you know what they say about time passing when you are having fun and all that,"

"Save it! I'm not in the mood right now, Ev."

"What is your problem? You need to relax."

"Relax? Really? You made us miss the boat back to the hotel, and now I can't get a signal out to call my husband and my children and let them know I'm ok. You are so inconsiderate sometimes; I swear you only think about yourself." As soon as she said the words, she regretted them. She loved her friend very much, and she never before had to talk to her in this manner.

"I'm glad I'm not married," Evelyn grimaced.

"Excuse me?" Camille asked.

"Nothing. Look I'm sorry, and you're right; we came on vacation together, and I should have been more considerate of your feelings, but you have to admit that after all I have been through, I need to have fun right now. Let's not argue tonight, please. I'm exhausted, and all I want to do is sleep."

"You're right, we shouldn't be arguing." Camille sighed and sat next to her friend on the bed. "I know that I shouldn't, but I do worry about you sometimes, no, all the time. You're more than just a friend, you are like a sister to me, and I don't want anything bad to happen to you; especially not while we are here. We are in a strange country with people we don't even know. I just think you should be more careful."

"And I appreciate that so much, and I am really having a good time; especially since I was almost attacked the first night that we came."

Before Evelyn could utter another word, Camille jumped what seemed like two feet off of the bed and into the air and stared at her friend.

"What?" Camille yelled. What do you mean you were attacked? When? Where? H-how?"

"Wait a minute, calm down girl before you get us in trouble with all this noise at this hour. See, I didn't want to tell you anything because I knew you would react like this."

Camille closed her eyes briefly and inhaled slowly, then exhaled out again. Then she opened her eyes, faked a little smile, and waited for Evelyn to tell her the story. Evelyn settled herself on the bed and tapped the side of the bed, motioning for her friend to sit.

She did.

"The night when we went down to the hotel bar, I met this guy, and we started talking, and he was telling me about the island. Then we decided to go for a walk, and that is when he tried..." Evelyn made air quotes-- "to attack me, but I handled it."

"Then what happened?" Camille said as calmly as she possibly could.

"I attacked him, took his wallet, and then left him there on the ground behind the hotel."

"Hold on," Camille said, putting up her hands. "Is this

the same wallet that I found on the floor in the hotel room?"

"Yes, it is."

Camille got up from the bed again. "Girl are you crazy. This man could have killed you!"

"And yet, he didn't," Evelyn said sarcastically.

Camille rubbed her forehead and started pacing the room. "At least please tell me the man isn't dead."

"Damn girl, I don't go around killing people. Who do you think I am, the Terminator?"

"Look at that; I can't even leave you alone for a minute." Camille sighed then they both laughed. "And that's what I'm talking about. You can't trust these people. If you had told me this before you know I would have never left you alone with that guy Anthony tonight, you're lucky he didn't try to hurt you too."

"Anthony is not like that."

"Really? And you know this how?"

"He's sweet and charming, and he makes me feel like no other man has ever made me feel before, just by his words."

"Sweet," Camille said, rolling her eyes. "Listen here, girly. We are leaving on the first thing smoking tomorrow morning, you hear me?"

"Yes, mother." She teased.

"But he is cute though," Evelyn said.

Camille shrugged.

As they were about to turn out the lights, Camille turned to Evelyn on the bed. It was a small room with a single full-size bed, not like the one back at the hotel with two huge queen size beds.

"So, what's he like?" she asked.

"What's who like?" Evelyn replied.

"Anthony,"

"Oh, he's really sweet, he knows how to talk to a woman and make her feel special. And the good thing about it, he doesn't seem clingy; he knows his boundaries, what to say and what not to say. He just knows how to keep your attention. And that accent, OMG!"

"Where's he from?"

"I think he said he was from Grenada, but I'm not sure."

"He sounds nice, does he have a girlfriend?"

"No, I don't think so, but he did say he had a roommate."

"I see." Camille said yawning, "I really want you to be happy Ev, just don't rush into anything ok?"

By the time Evelyn looked across at her friend to give an answer, she had already fallen asleep and had begun to snore. She smiled to herself. She picked up her phone and sent a message to Anthony that she had a wonderful time chatting with him and looked forward to seeing him the next day when he takes them for breakfast, something she had forgotten to tell Camille.

When he didn't respond, she turned on her side towards her best friend and watched her while she slept. She realized that she was right about one thing, they were in a strange country, and anything could happen there. She made a vow to herself that she was going to be cautious for the next couple of days that they were going to be on vacation.

While talking to Camille about the attack, she remembered that she never mentioned to her that there was another guy there, the same guy that she had spotted back at the airport. She didn't want to tell Camille about him until she knew why he was there and what he wanted. She knew that her friend would worry; hell, she might even catch the next flight back home. She was going to make sure that she found out who he was, where he was staying, and why he was following her. But for now, she was going to enjoy this trip and live in the moment.

The phone buzzed, and she opened it thinking it was Anthony, but the number was blocked, and she gasped when she saw the message.

Have a good night beautiful
My sweet black rose

CHAPTER 10

HE WOKE UP THE NEXT MORNING, AND AS USUAL, HE listened with his ear against the wall to the adjacent room where the women stayed. Nothing. Now he was starting to get worried. He hadn't heard anything from their room yesterday, and now he still wasn't hearing any sounds. He didn't know how he had missed them.

There were no movements in the room next door, no talking, no whispering, just quiet. So how did he miss them? He paced the room, wondering what to do or where to go next.

Had he overslept? No. When he moved the blinds to the window slightly, he discovered it was still dark out, and the digital clock on the nightstand next to his bed revealed it was 5:15 am. He was suddenly in desperate need of coffee and food and decided to put on the coffee pot and wait until it was a little brighter outside to get food. His stomach growled a bit, and he had nothing in his room to eat, and the hotel breakfast did not come out until 7 a.m.

At this point, he figured that the ladies may still be sleeping, or hungover from drinking or partying all night. When the pot stopped brewing, he poured himself a cup of coffee and sat in the chair next to the window and waited until he heard a noise coming from the next room.

Minutes later, he dozed off a bit, and when he awoke two hours later, he listened again, but he still heard nothing coming from the room next door. No voices, no TV; it was a ghost town next door. The only other option was to call the front desk and see if they had checked out already. He was going to kick himself if they did.

He decided to leave the room and head downstairs to the lobby and wait for them to come down and get breakfast because he was hungry. All he had to eat for the past couple of days was fruit, coconut water, and a bottle of rum from the bar downstairs.

He left his room and walked down the hall towards the ladies' room door and saw the complimentary newspaper still sitting on the mat. No one had picked it up yet. Were they still asleep? He slowly walked by listening carefully for any footsteps or anything that might indicate some kind of movement.

Again, nothing.

The elevator dinged, and he quickly entered, hitting the ground floor button. When the elevator reached the lobby, he carefully exited just in case he spotted them. When he didn't, the man sat and waited by the breakfast area where he got some fruit, a bagel with jam, and poured himself another cup of coffee. He sat close enough where he had a perfect vantage point to the elevator but not too close that they spotted him.

He took a newspaper that someone had left from the table next to him and pretended to read it by glancing up a few times when he heard the elevator.

At 10:00 a.m., the breakfast area in the lobby was beginning to clear, and he realized then that the ladies were never going to come down. Where the hell were they? He glanced around a few times to see if he could spot them then he slowly got up from the table, and casually walked over to the elevator and hit his floor. His heart leaped when the elevator slowly opened, and the laughter of women came through. But to his dismay, it wasn't them. What was going on?

He remembered overhearing them the day before saying that they were going to go sightseeing, but he had assumed that they would be back by now. When the elevator got to his floor, he emerged slowly, holding up the newspaper to be cautious, just in case he ran into them. He again walked quietly past their room door, as he had hours before, and listened for any signs of activity. There were none.

Had the woman made him out? Maybe.

He knew Evelyn was very smart and she left no stone unturned, she might have been lousy at life, but she was a brilliant detective. Yes, he knew her very well. He knew about her past. He knew that she was married before, he knew that her husband had died, and he knew that she claimed self-defense in his death, which didn't allow her any jail time. He had known about the bruises, the broken rib, the times she spent in the hospital. He knew about her parents; her mother had a bad heart, and her father had left them; he didn't know why, and he didn't care. He knew about her abandonment issues. He had seen enough psychologists to know that her father abandoning her made her a target for abusive relationships. The only thing he didn't know right now, was where the hell they were, and how had he let them slip past him?

He went back to his hotel room and slammed the door so hard it almost came off the hinges. He shouldn't have done that, and now he was getting one of his headaches again.

"Dammit," he screamed.

He began to feel slightly dizzy and scratched his head; had he messed up again? No, but something wasn't right; why hadn't he heard them leave the room? He tried to retrace his steps. The last time he saw them was two days ago in the lobby talking to a guy, a tour guide maybe, he wasn't sure. He noticed Evelyn turned in his direction, and he spun around and pretended to start reading a magazine that was on a nearby rack. When he turned back again, they were gone. He didn't see where they went. Did they get into the taxi? Crap! He was starting to mess up. He went to the nearby bar, and he couldn't remember anything after that.

He paced the room again, and that's when he saw it, the empty rum bottle on the floor next to his bed. Had he drunk himself to sleep again? He couldn't remember.

"Think dammit!" he said.

He thought for a moment. Then he was about to pick up his cell phone and call his employer when he heard faint laughter coming from what sounded like women walking in the hallway. He quickly headed over to the door and looked through the peephole, but it wasn't them.

He had to think fast. The only other thing he could do was to break into the ladies' room and make sure that they were both still on the island.

Then he heard the vacuum next door and realized that the maid must have started cleaning the rooms. He decided that he would take that opportunity to sneak into the room and look around, and then leave before anyone became suspicious.

The man patiently waited until he heard the maid cleaning the room on the other side of him; then he slowly opened his room door and paced the hall. Then he saw a master key on the cart and took it before she came out of the room. After the maid emerged from the room, he took that opportunity to slip past her and quickly ducked behind the door. It all happened in what seemed like mere seconds.

The first thing that he saw was the women's suitcases by their beds. He smiled to himself as his surveillance was back on. They hadn't left yet, and that was a good thing, he thought to himself. But what he thought of next was something short of pure genius, and he smiled.

CHAPTER 11

THE NEXT DAY EVELYN AND CAMILLE CAUGHT A TAXI which took them to a local restaurant for breakfast. Evelyn ordered a Mediterranean omelet with plantains and toast, and Camille ordered the French toast with scrambled eggs. The food was amazing, and Evelyn wanted to meet the chef who she was told was Julie McKay. When the chef came out of the kitchen to meet them, they introduced themselves to her.

"This is awesome, I haven't had breakfast quite like this before, and the seasonings are just perfect," Evelyn said.

"Thank you so much, are you here on vacation?" the chef asked.

"Yes," Camille said, "this is our first time here, and we are having a blast." Camille glanced over at Evelyn, who was suddenly staring at the chef with her brows narrowed as if she had seen something familiar.

Camille gently kicked her friend under the table, and

she jumped a little. "Yes, this is our first time," Evelyn said as she cleared her throat. The chef smiled at them again.

"Well, I'm sorry ladies, but I have to go back into the kitchen now, it was so nice meeting you."

"You too," the ladies said in unison.

As soon as the chef was out of sight, Camille gave Evelyn a little pinch on her arm. "What is wrong with you? Why were you staring at the lady like that?"

"You didn't hear that accent?"

"Yea, so what?"

"Oh, never mind." Evelyn said, "It's nothing."

"Talking about accent, wasn't your boyfriend Anthony supposed to meet us here?" Camille asked.

Evelyn had texted Anthony before she left the hotel that they were going to have breakfast, and he agreed to meet them. Evelyn texted Anthony and told him where they were, and he told her he would meet them outside after they had breakfast.

"He was, but he had some things to do today," Evelyn said. Are you going to spend the day with us?"

"Of course, what kind of friend would I be if I left you alone over here on this island where we don't know anyone?"

"We know Anthony..."

"Excuse me; you know Anthony? Barely," Camille said, rolling her eyes. But that didn't faze Evelyn, she just smiled.

Camille started sipping on her orange juice and looked like her mind was on something else. She was staring blankly into the glass and stirring it with her straw.

"What's the matter, Hun? Are you still thinking about your husband and kids? I promise that we will go back over to the hotel after we are finished here."

"No, no. It's not that. There's just something that I have to tell you that I should have told you last night." Camille said.

"What?"

"I spoke to Richard last night while you and Anthony were downstairs talking."

"Okay?" Evelyn said, waiting for her friend to continue.

"Well... I got a message on my phone, and when I saw it was him, I called him back because I thought it was an emergency with my husband or my kids..."

"Girl, just say it. What did Richard want?"

"Well-" Camille paused, "He was concerned about you, and he wanted to know if everything was okay. He said the last time you guys spoke, you were angry with him."

"Unbelievable!" Evelyn said, throwing up her hands in the air. "This guy never gives up, does he? I just can't seem to get a break." She sighed. "Is that why you were pacing and talking to yourself when I came in?"

Camille nodded. "I'm sorry, I should have told you."

"No, it's fine. I just can't believe this guy sometimes."

"Why don't you give him another chance Ev? He's such a nice and caring guy, he just doesn't want anything bad to happen to you, and neither do I."

"No, no, and no; and for this very same reason. You don't know him, Cam. He's so clingy; he has to know where I am every minute of every day... what I am doing. It's exhausting. He's exhausting! I can't deal with it. He clearly doesn't know what boundaries are. He reminds me of my ex-husband."

Camille looked at Evelyn and felt as if someone had just slapped her in the face to wake her from a dream she was having. Only it wasn't a dream.

"Wait, wait, what the hell did you just say?" Camille asked.

"Yes, I was married before, a long time ago."

Camille eased over and playfully nudged her friend on the arm and pulled her chair closer to hers.

"Details, child, I need details. Who was he? Was he cute? Where's he now?"

"Well, he's dead," Evelyn said matter-of-factly.

Camille straightened and stared at Evelyn then she leaned into her friend and hugged her shoulders. "Girl, I'm so sorry."

"Yup, I killed him, Cam."

Another proverbial slap in the face and this time she was awakened for sure. Camille eased back in her chair and stared at her friend. This was all news to her. She knew that there were some things that Evelyn was keeping from her when they met, but nothing so severe, so sinister had ever crossed her mind. Who was Evelyn Rose Dubois really? She killed her husband? What was she about to tell Camille next? All this was getting insane. Camille was in such shock that the words that were entering her mind could not get to her lips, and all she could do at that moment was to sip on her juice.

Evelyn cleared her throat and then began to tell Camille what happened.

"As I said before, it was a long time ago before you and I met. I met this guy; he was gorgeous, charming, caring, loving, everything that I ever prayed for in a guy. He was it. Until he slowly began to change, and I became his human punching bag."

Camille nodded but stayed quiet.

"I was living in hell. I couldn't tell my mom; you know she was sick with her heart, and I didn't want her to worry and make things worse. I couldn't tell anyone. I felt weak and ashamed. And I held on to that secret for years."

Camille held her friend's hand now and blinked back tears from her eyes.

"A couple of times, I ended up in the hospital with a broken wrist, broken ribs, a black eye. I got the courage, and I fought back, but it only made things even worse, so I packed my bags one day, and I left. I ran away."

"Good for you, hun."

"Wait. Then he found me, kidnapped me, beat me up, and left me for dead. For days, I was tied up with little or nothing to eat or drink — blood all over my clothes. I get nightmares about it until this very day. But one day, while still tied up, I said to myself, No, I'm not going to die here, not today. I ended up killing him."

"I'm sorry, so sorry that happened to you. I'm so sorry." Camille leaned in again and hugged her. "I had no idea you had to go through something so horrible; I don't know what to say."

"It's okay. I will be alright. Just promise me you won't tell anyone that I told you this? I don't even want Richard to know. You already know how he gets about me."

"Don't you think he already knows? He works for the damn FBI," Camille said, and they both laughed at that.

They were laughing so hard and talking so much that Evelyn didn't hear her phone buzz several times next to her. When she finally looked at it, she saw that there were several messages from Anthony.

When Anthony finally showed up at the restaurant, they went with him in his jeep, and they spent the day driving around the island. They enjoyed each other's company, but Evelyn and Camille had to catch the boat at 4:30 p.m. to head back to the hotel so that Camille could call her husband and check up on the kids. Evelyn didn't want to leave, but what kind of friend would she be if she let her friend go back to the hotel alone. She told Anthony that she would text him and that they would stay in contact.

Hours later, Evelyn and Camille returned to their hotel room, still laughing and reminiscing about their day. As soon as Evelyn opened the door, she noticed a long silver box, wrapped with a beautiful red ribbon, sitting on the desk.

Without considering who had sent it or even how it might have gotten into the room, Camille rushed past her and picked it up. "Oooh, girl I wonder who these are from? Could it be from Richard? Or wait, maybe Anthony? Girl, open the box. Let's see!"

Evelyn shook her head and took the package from Camille. "You are so silly."

Grinning, she removed the card from underneath the huge satin bow and set it back onto the desk before unwrapping the ribbon and opening the box.

Immediately, Evelyn froze. She didn't say anything, just stared at the contents inside.

Concerned, Camille quickly glanced into the box, but as soon as she saw what was in it, she also froze. They both looked at each other. Inside Evelyn's box were a dozen Roses.

Black Roses.

Evelyn's mind quickly returned to the day that the single black rose had been left in front of the hotel room door. What could this mean? Who would send her black roses?

Retrieving the small white envelope from the desk, she opened the envelope and read the card:

RIP Evelyn Rose Dubois

CHAPTER 12

Claude Amos, the man hired to follow Evelyn and Camille to St. Thomas, sat in the lobby and waited and watched as the women exited the taxi and headed towards the lobby to the elevators. They were laughing and talking as the elevator opened and then closed behind them and rose to the fourth floor.

He had been waiting all day and was about to give up and head back upstairs when he noticed a taxi pull up. Now his plans were back as usual, but then again sending those roses to the women's room was nothing short of genius. He wished he was there to see their faces, again.

He needed a drink.

Getting up from his chair and looking around the room, he walked to the hotel bar and took a seat at the edge so that no one else would bother him. He needed some time to himself, plus he was not a people person anyway. He didn't like making small talk with strangers. He was here for a mission and not to make friends.

He was now thinking about the box of a dozen black roses that he had sent to the ladies' room. He made sure and put them in the room himself this time. That was hours before they came back from wherever they had been for the past two days. He had to stifle back a grin so that people wouldn't think he was a crazy guy sitting by himself and grinning like a fool. What did he care?

He pounded the bar with his palm, "Hey man, a beer over here," he mumbled to the bartender. He looked around the room until his gaze settled on the television screen above the bar. The place wasn't full at this hour; it was still early. There were a few tourists and locals sitting at the bar talking to each other about a game or a fight. He didn't know. He didn't care.

"Here you go man," the bartender said, handing him a cold beer. He sipped it and turned his gaze back to the TV.

He felt his phone buzz in his pocket and took it out and stared at it. He cursed under his breath. His employer had sent him a text message. He hadn't contacted him in a while, because he had nothing new to tell him. He placed the phone back in his pocket and continued to watch the overhead screen and sip on his beer.

A lady sat on the stool next to him. She was alone and reminded him a little bit of Evelyn. He thought about the first time he actually saw Evelyn, he followed her that night from her job, then to the gym, then home. He hid outside her house close enough that he could see inside through the windows. He crouched down behind some shrubs so as to not be seen by the neighbors or someone passing by. He watched her for most of the night, and he watched as she walked around the kitchen with the phone glued to her ear. He watched as she went from the fridge to the stove to the island. She looked like she was cooking dinner.

A loud noise startled him and immediately put him on edge. Had he gotten caught? He cursed under his breath. After a few long and tense seconds, he slowly turned in the direction of the noise and saw a black cat emerge from the bushes and sprinted across the lawn as if something had chased it. Another string of curses escaped his lips, and he finally took in a deep breath.

He rubbed his eyes. He was starting to get tired, and he felt the beginnings of one of his headaches, but he tried to ignore it since it could serve as a distraction to his mission.

He waited patiently for about another hour, his legs were beginning to get numb, and his eyes were heavy from sleep depravity.

"Come on, man. Don't fall asleep now." He scolded himself.

Hours later and Evelyn still had not gone to bed yet; she had moved to the living room and was now sitting on the couch with her laptop. The television was on, and he watched as she sipped her glass filled with wine.

He waited still until he saw the lights in both rooms go off. Figuring the object of his mission was tired and had gone to bed, he made his way closer to the house. Looking around once more to make sure that no one was in the area, he made sure to take careful steps towards the back of the house.

"Hey, you. Get out of there!" he heard a woman scream from behind him.

He froze. Then looked around in the direction of the woman's voice.

"Did you hear me? Don't let me come in there and get you. Get out of there right this minute." She said again.

He let out a relieved breath. The woman was talking to someone inside her house.

"Get it together, man," he mumbled under his breath.

He walked up the stone walkway, lightly stepped onto the wooden deck to the glass-paned porch door, and carefully turned the knob. It was locked.

Suddenly there was a light from the street, and a car turned slowly in his direction stopped and parked. He ducked quickly behind a garbage can that was next to the back door. Then the light in the house went on, and the car door opened and closed.

"What now?" he whispered.

A tall, dark man about 6 feet stepped out of the car and walked up the concrete path towards the front of the house. He heard voices, a woman then a man and then laughter followed. He wanted to raise his head a bit and peek through the window, but it was too risky, they would see him. Minutes later, the light in the living room went off then the other light that came on, he assumed it was from the bedroom.

His plan and his night were ruined by Evelyn's boyfriend, there had to be another way, but first, he had to make it back to his car without being seen. He casually walked back in the direction from which he came, glancing at the car's license plate and memorizing it.

He waited to see if the mysterious man would come out of the house and after an hour later there was still no movement the house. He had given up on waiting for the man to leave.

He took out his laptop and punched some keys, making a note to find out who the owner of the car was. His new mission now was to follow him and get to know him, so he could get to Evelyn.

CHAPTER 13

A COUPLE OF WEEKS EARLIER, RICHARD LEFT HIS office at 6:30 p.m., got into his white BMW, and made his way to the gym to meet up with his college buddies. Hitting the seek button, he found a song that he liked and then started singing along to a classic in a high pitched out of tune voice, with his hands every so often swaying back and forth in the air.

Richard Elias hadn't noticed the black SUV tailing him when he left the office, nor did he notice it swerving in and out of traffic trying to catch up to him; he was busy singing along to the music on his car radio. He was heading to the gym; he was starting to feel a little pouch in his mid-section lately, and he had to get back on track.

Pulling up in the parking lot of the gym, the dark SUV pulled in behind him and parked a distance away. Richard got out of his car with his gym bag, locked it, and walked to the entrance still humming the music that had been playing in his car.

"Hey Rich, I haven't seen you here in a while, where you been?" a guy said to him heading out of the door.

"You know I been busy at work; I got to catch up to you now, huh?"

The man put a thumb up and hustled to the parking lot. He met with some of his friends and worked out for about an hour and a half before leaving the gym and heading outside with one of his buddies.

"So that new chic is the reason why you haven't been to the gym lately? How is she anyway?" his friend said.

"No." He chuckled, "I've just been busy with a lot of cases, but Evelyn is good."

"Oh, so she does have a name. When are we going to meet her?"

"I know how you guys are. I'm never bringing her around you," Richard teased, "You might taint her image of me." They both laughed.

"Okay man, I got to run."

"Cool, see you next week?"

"Next week," he yelled back as he jogged towards his car.

When Richard got to his car, he used his cell phone light to see in the now dark parking when he noticed that his front tire was flat.

"Shit," he screamed. He walked around the other side of the car and noticed that the other front tire was flat too. As a matter of fact, all four tires were flat, right down to the rim.

* * *

Following Richard Elias was easy and finding out who he was, was even easier. Claude found out his name and address at the DMV after he told them that he had hit his car and wanted his name and address so that he could repay him. Now it was time to befriend him.

Richard's daily routine was somewhat simple, work, home and the occasional stop at the grocery store and of course the occasional rendezvous at Evelyn's House. He wondered how long that relationship was going on, but quickly threw that thought right out of his mind. The only thing he cared about was getting to Evelyn, and if he had to eliminate some problems to get to her, so be it.

He had followed Richard to the Gym and parked several feet away so that he didn't notice him. After all, he was an FBI agent. He had planned it so well when Richard came out and found his tires had been flat. He knows that flattening all of the tires would be a bit much, but what the hell. He would sneak up behind him in the dark, drug him and take him back to his vehicle and drive away and no one would see.

Claude got out of the vehicle and watched as Richard made several trips around it, not sure of what to do next; then he took out his cell phone and punched it. He slowly walked over to Richard.

"Hey man, you need some help there?" Claude asked, quickly thinking when Richard turned in his direction.

"Yea, I can't believe it, I don't understand how all four tires could be flat at the same time. I just bought two new tires last week." Richard said, scratching his head.

"I have some tools in the back of my truck if you need a hand with that."

"No, I think I'll be fine. I'll just call AAA or leave the car here until the morning."

"Come on, I think I have some plugs in the back I can help you fix it, and then you can drive right to your garage tonight."

Richard thought for a minute, "Oh, Okay. But I owe you, man."

"Hey, don't worry about it."

It had taken them an hour and a half, but the two men took off each tire one by one, plugged it and inflated them with a portable inflator and replaced them on the car.

"Thanks again, man. I don't know what I would have done if you didn't come along when you did."

"It's no problem, forget about it."

"Well at least let me buy you a drink, there's a bar not too far down the road, we can stop there for a couple of minutes. This is just my way of saying thanks," Richard said

"Okay, no problem," Claude said.

They each drove their own vehicles to the bar that was ten minutes away from the gym. Richard had changed from a gym shirt into an extra shirt that he carried in his bag.

They both entered the bar and found two seats at the counter.

"This is a nice place," Clause said, looking around the room. "I don't think I have been in here before."

"Yea, it's pretty cool, my friends and I come here a lot after work just to kick back and relax, but we haven't been able to in the last couple days, I have been so tied up at work," Richard said.

Claude turned and banged on the counter to get the attention of the bartender.

"A beer for me and my friend here," He said.

He put out his hand to greet Richard "By the way, my name is Claude."

"I'm Richard. Nice to meet you, man."

Richard did something that he never did in his entire life; he had sat down and had drinks with Evelyn's future murderer.

CHAPTER 14

"WHO DO YOU THINK THESE CAME FROM EVELYN?"
She said, still staring at the box of roses.

"I don't know who sent these roses; maybe it was a
mistake or a joke," Evelyn said. She wasn't sure who had
sent them, but she had an idea. The next step was to find
out why.

"What is going on today? One, with you being
married, the other, getting mysterious packages assuming
you're dead. I don't know how much more I can take, girl."

"It's probably a mistake as I said. Don't worry
about it."

"Okay, well we only have another week here so, I'm
glad we'll be leaving soon." Her friend said, but she wasn't
stupid, she sensed that something was definitely off.

"About that," Evelyn said.

"Oh no, don't tell me. Please don't tell me."

"I think I will stay a little longer; I like it here."

"I'm not leaving you here by yourself, Evelyn. Hell no, definitely not," Camille said.

"I'll be fine. Plus, I will be with Anthony, and you know how nice he is; he won't let anything happen to me. I will be fine."

"Hmm, sure you will," Camille said sarcastically. "I'm tired, I'm going to take a long shower and call my husband and my kids, then go to bed. It doesn't make sense to argue with you."

Evelyn didn't respond; she was too busy thinking about how she was going to approach him. The man who had been following her, at home, to work, at the airport, and now he was here on what was supposed to be her vacation. The only thing she didn't know was what he wanted and who sent him. While he was doing his investigations on her, she was doing the same thing on him. She was too smart for him. His name she didn't know yet, but she would find out soon enough. She had put her plan into action in her mind. Finding out what room he was staying in would be tricky, but it would be the next step.

Camille emerged from the bathroom in her bathrobe with the phone plastered to her ear, talking to her husband. Evelyn took this time to grab her towel and robe and take a hot shower. As she stepped into the shower and let the water flow down her back, she began to reminisce about her time on the island. She thought about Anthony and wondered what it was like to spend the entire day with him, alone. She wondered what his lips would feel like against her lips, her body. She imagined him touching her slowly along the length of her body, softly kissing every spot that he touched. It was an image that she hoped would soon come true.

When Evelyn went back into the room, she found Camille watching the TV with her eyes wide and mouth open.

"Girl, Ev look at this." She said.

"What?" Evelyn went over to the bed and sat down next to her friend who was watching a news report on the television.

"Body of a young local was found this evening washed up on the shore of a local beach," the newswoman said. "He was found by tourist as they were taking a stroll on the beach. His body appeared to be badly beaten," She continued.

Then there was a picture shown in the upper left corner of the television screen of a man she soon recognized, and Evelyn gasped. It was the guy whom she had met at the bar the first night that she came to the Island. She side-eyed her friend, who was so intently watching the news that she didn't notice her panic.

Evelyn had forgotten to get rid of the wallet.

What would be her explanation if the police suddenly came to search the room? Was she the last person to see him that night? Would they even come? Questions raced through her mind.

"His wife had reported him missing a few days ago to the local authorities and said that he went out to a business meeting and never returned home. Anyone who has information about this man, please contact the proper authorities." the woman on the screen continued.

Camille switched off the television and turned to Evelyn who was still staring blankly at the now dark screen.

"Can you believe that? That's terrible; I hope they find out who did it. Now I'm getting nervous, can you imagine that man was at this very hotel? I'm sorry, but I won't be going anywhere alone from now on. And you better not either."

"Relax, maybe he just pissed someone off, maybe he owed them money or into drugs or something. We came here to have some fun so don't let a little news scare you, ok?"

Evelyn noticed that her friend was starting to nestle under the covers. "Wait, what are you doing?"

"I'm tired; I'm going to sleep."

"Girl, it's still early. Let's go down to the bar and get a drink," Evelyn said.

"No, I think I'll call it a day and just get some rest."

"Okay. Well, I think I will get some rest too," Evelyn lied. She would wait until her friend was in a deep sleep before sneaking out to the bar. She didn't have to wait long. An hour later, she was dressed. She grabbed the man's wallet from inside of the dresser put it into her bag, and quietly left the hotel room.

* * * *

"Anything good here?" the woman who sat down next to Claude asked.

He was about to turn and say something, but when

he saw her, he knocked over his beer and quickly grabbed a nearby napkin to wipe it up. The woman giggled slightly and tapped the bar to get the bartender's attention.

"Hey, one beer for me and one for my friend here please." She said then turned back to the man and watched as he nervously wiped up the mess that he had made.

"So," she continued. "You like it here? The place is nice, isn't it?"

The man nodded. "It's alright, I guess." He shrugged.

"I know that accent, you're not from here, are you? Are you here on vacation too?"

"Not really, it's more of a business trip." He said as he cleared his throat.

When the bartender brought over the beers, he quickly took one and mumbled a thank you towards the woman. She sipped on her beer and casually looked around the room.

"I'm sorry where are my manners I didn't introduce myself, my name is Evelyn, Evelyn Rose." She said, holding out a hand for him to shake it.

"Nice to meet you," he said in a low grumble then he turned and took her hand, barely shaking it, and turned back to watch TV. It took all of him not to make a mistake and say, 'I know you are.' He tried to keep his cool. What was she doing here, anyway? What was her game? Did she know who he was?

Evelyn paused for a second when he spoke; she thought she recognized his accent, the way that he said certain things. Where had she heard it before? Was he hiding his voice?

"Do you have a name?" she asked.

He turned and looked at her for a moment before answering. Did he want to tell her his real name? It didn't matter because she wasn't going to live long enough to remember it. He stared at her now; he hadn't realized how beautiful this woman was up close. She flicked back a loose strand of her hair and smiled at him. He noticed that her hair was shiny, black with a hint of brown highlights. She obviously washed it today, a couple of hours ago maybe, she was even wearing makeup which she clearly didn't need. He wanted to tell her how beautiful she was.

Focus.

"It's Claude," He said.

"Nice to meet you, Claude. Are you here alone or did you come with your family?"

"As I said before, I'm here on business, so I came alone," he said.

"That's right," she said, sipping her beer. "I love it here. It's so beautiful, and the beaches are so pristine; I've never seen water so blue in all my life. Well, except in magazines and on the internet. I wish I could stay here forever; unfortunately, I have to go back to work soon. What about you? What kind of work you do?"

"You really do ask a lot of questions, Ms. Rose."

Her smile was now gone as she leaned forward in her chair and took in a whiff of his cologne. The scent had taken her by surprise; it was so familiar. Who was this guy?

"I'm sorry. Well, wait. I do have one more question for you, Claude." she said.

"Oh, Yea? And what's that?" he asked her.

"Why the hell are you following me?"

CHAPTER 15

"So, you know who I am?"

It was pure luck that Evelyn just happened to be at the bar at the same time that this man, the man who had followed her all the way to St. Thomas, was there.

"Not really, but I know you've been following me. Tell me how long it has been? Weeks? Months? I want to know why? Why are you here in St. Thomas and who sent you?"

"Well, you see, if I tell you that I might have to kill you," He laughed.

"Ha. I'm pretty sure if you wanted to kill me, you would have done that already; you wouldn't have followed me all the way here. You're either a lousy spy or a stupid one. So, tell me who sent you? Who's paying you?"

"Maybe you should ask your boyfriend." He said, glaring at her.

"My boyfriend," she replied, seemingly confused for a

moment. "Richard? Are you telling me that Richard hired you to follow me? That bastard," she mumbled under her breath. "How much is he paying you to keep your eyes on me?"

"What makes you think he doesn't want you dead?"

"Because I know him," she stated while plastering a fake smile on her face and taking a sip of her beer. She would call Richard and deal with him later, but for now, she wanted to know more about this guy and why he wanted her dead.

"Did he call you and warn you about me?" the man asked her.

"No."

"Well, what kind of game are you playing?"

"No games. How much is he paying you?"

"A whole lot of money," when he said it this time he wasn't smiling. He slammed his hand on the bar to get the bartender's attention again. "Another beer for me and one for the lady here."

Evelyn waved off the bartender, "Nothing for me, thanks."

They waited until the guy brought over the beer and set in down in front of Claude. He took a sip of it, and for a moment, there was silence.

"I'll double your price." Evelyn finally said, easing closer to the man as he inhaled a whiff of her perfume.

"What?" the man said, slowly taking in her scent. She was beautiful, he thought to himself, and she smelled good too. But he had to stay focused.

"Whatever he is paying you, I'll double it; and I want

you to leave the island immediately and never follow me again."

"And why would I do that?" he laughed.

"Because, unlike you, I consider myself very smart and seeing that it didn't take me long to figure out what you were up to and—" she gestured with her hands open, "where to find you...You are sloppy, and I knew that eventually, you would slip up. So, it's up to you. Either you're going to get out of here by tomorrow, or you'll end up missing. Oh, just like your friend there on the news earlier tonight? You didn't think I knew it was you? Leave now, or I will make your life a living hell."

The man threw his head back and laughed uncontrollably. The music was loud, and as there were only a few people, mostly tourists, engaged in conversations at tables scattered throughout the bar or on the dance floor, no one even noticed.

"You should really consider leaving your current job and taking up comedy," he said.

"So, you think this is funny?"

"I do," the man said. "But I must say I didn't know you would be so beautiful, or I would have killed you a long time ago and collected my money."

More patrons were starting to come into the bar, and the music seemed to get louder and louder.

"So how did you find me, by the way?" the man leaned into Evelyn and tried to talk over the music.

"As I said, you are pretty lousy," she said in a mocking voice. She waved the bartender over this time.

"Another beer?" The bartender asked her.

"No, let me have a rum and coke, please." She turned back to Claude, "If I have to sit here and listen to you, I'm going to need something a little stronger."

The man eased over his stool a bit closer to Evelyn. "Why would someone want to kill such a beautiful woman as yourself? You know you deserve better than that creep."

"He's not the one that wants me dead, you are. And I want to know why?"

"Oh right, silly me," He said as he tapped his forehead with his hand.

The man ordered another beer, then another, then another and one by one she watched as he slurped them down quickly. Then she realized that he was getting drunk. He obviously could not control his alcohol.

She looked down and happened to see something peering out of his pocket, his room key. She had to grab it without him knowing. She wanted to get back to his room and look around a bit to see what he was up to.

Eight beers and several shots later, and Claude was rocking back and forth swaying uncontrollably to the music; he was definitely drunk, and Evelyn had him exactly where she wanted him, vulnerable.

When he could no longer stand comfortably on both feet without falling over, Evelyn decided to take him up to his room.

"Ok now, I think you've had enough to drink for tonight, what room are you in?" she asked him.

"Room 414," he answered, slurring his words.

"That bastard," she thought to herself, they were in

415. The man was in the room right next to hers; he must have been listening to their conversations and studying their every move. That made her furious.

They made their way to the elevator, pressed the button for the 4th floor, then she dragged the now half-sleep half-awake body to his room, took his room key from his pocket and opened the door. She then threw him onto the bed and sat in a nearby chair to catch her breath.

She waited a few minutes until she heard him snoring then she started looking quietly around the room. She searched for a suitcase but only found an overnight bag. There wasn't much inside this bag except for some clothes and toiletries.

"There has to be something," she whispered to herself.

She began to search his pockets and found his cell phone. It was unlocked, so she began to go through it. There was only one number on it; she didn't recognize it, but she dialed it anyway.

When the person on the other line answered, she instantly recognized the voice.

"Well, hello there, lover. Or, should I say, ex-lover," She said.

"Evelyn? What the-" Richard said surprised.

"Don't even act surprised. I know everything. Your little errand boy here spilled his guts and told me every-thing. How could you pay this idiot to follow me, are you out of your ever-loving mind?"

"Wait, let me explain."

"Nope! No explanations necessary, Richard."

"At least tell me this," he interrupted.

"What?"

"Is he dead?"

"Well, he's unconscious, for now."

"Oh my God Evelyn, what did you do?"

"What kind of woman do you think I am? I haven't done anything to him; he's drunk, and I brought him back to his room. Well, after I slipped a little something into his beer. He'll sleep until morning."

She heard Richard sigh on the other end of the call.

"Oh, you're not quite off the hook yet buddy. Just wait until I get back home. Since you want to talk, I have a whole lot to say to you," she said, before hanging up the phone. She was more upset now than she had been when she found out that Richard had hired Claude to follow her to the Caribbean. One thing she was certain of, he hadn't hired this maniac to kill her.

So, who did?

That was what she had to find out. But for now, she was going to stay right here and wait until he woke up.

CHAPTER 16

A COUPLE OF HOURS LATER, EVELYN WENT BACK TO her room to make sure that Camille hadn't woken up during the night and started to worry about her. But when she opened the door, Camille was awake and frantic on the phone.

"Oh, my God, girl! I'm sorry. I was bored, and I just went to the bar for a drink and time got away from me."

Camille put her hands to her lips while still listening on the call. This made Evelyn worried. She hurried over to her friend and sat next to her on the bed. Camille was on the phone with the airline and was trying to get the next flight out of St. Thomas. When the woman finally told her that she could put her on the next flight, which left at 1 p.m. the next day, she hung up.

"What's up, Cam?" Evelyn asked.

"Joe and the girls got into a wreck, and I have to leave. I'm sorry we have to cut this trip short, but I have to go home to my family."

"I understand, is anybody hurt, are they at the hospital?"

"No, they're fine, thank God, but the whole thing got me so shaken up. Apparently, Joe was heading home after getting the girls up from my mom's house, and he wanted to stop by the corner store for some groceries before heading home. Just as he stopped the car and put it into park, a group of young guys ran out of the place and apparently one of them had a gun. So, he shouted at the girls to duck, then a guy in the car in front of him reversed and slammed right into Joe's car and sped away. I guess he was frightened or something. But the airbags deployed, and Joe hurt his neck and his back. It's not serious, but I really need to go home and make sure that everyone is ok."

"Okay, but when did this happen?"

"About two hours ago. Joe was trying to reach me, but I was sleeping and didn't hear the phone ringing. So, when I got up to use the bathroom, I checked my phone, and I saw several missed calls, plus messages from Joe. He had me so frightened that I forgot I had to pee." They both laughed. "So where were you tonight?"

Evelyn lied. "I got bored, so I went down to the bar for a while." She then got up from the bed when her friend stopped her.

"Ev, I need you to come with me tomorrow. I can call the airline back and see if I can get you on the flight."

"Don't be silly; I will be alright."

"Are you sure?"

"Yes, I'll be fine," Evelyn said.

She wasn't worried about the man in the other room. He wasn't going to wake up anytime soon, but when he did, he was going to have one hell of a headache.

"Get some sleep Cam, everything will be alright," she told her friend.

"Yeah, I know."

* * *

The next morning at 7:30 am, Camille woke up, showered, dressed, and began packing her bags to catch the next flight out. Evelyn wasn't in her bed, and she thought that she must have gone down to get breakfast. She felt bad because she didn't want to leave Evelyn alone in a country where she didn't know anyone.

Camille knew that Evelyn was not about to leave without saying goodbye to Anthony, and there was no sense in arguing with her. A few minutes later, Evelyn entered the room with two coffees in her hand.

"All set?" she asked her friend, handing her a coffee cup.

"I think you should come home with me Evelyn; I don't feel comfortable leaving you here by yourself."

"Let's not do this again okay; I'm a big girl. I'll be fine," she said reassuringly, before telling her friend that she was going to see Anthony again.

"Have you spoken to him since you got back over?"

"I sent him a text earlier, but he hasn't responded yet."

Camille didn't like Anthony, she was very suspicious of him, and her suspicions were usually right.

"You need to leave that one there alone and come back with me. Richard would be very worried about you," She said.

But Evelyn wasn't thinking about Richard; the only man she had on her mind was Anthony. She had to see him again, and that was exactly what she was going to do.

"I'm not thinking about him right now; you just have a safe flight and go see about your family, okay? Does Joe know you're coming?"

"Yeah, I called him this morning, he's going to meet me when I land in a couple of hours."

"Well, tell him I said hi and kiss the girls for me, okay? And don't worry about me. You are my little worry-wart; you know that?"

"Funny," Camille said.

When Camille left for the airport, Evelyn took a shower and sent Anthony another text message. But still, there was no answer. She had to go back to the room next door to check up on Claude.

Earlier that morning, before Camille had gotten up, she had gone to check on him. He was still fast asleep, and she wanted to make sure of that; but just in case he woke up when she was gone, she had used one of his shirts and tied his hands to the bedposts. She wasn't sure when the tablets would wear off. They were the sleeping pills that the doctor had prescribed to her whenever she got anxious, and they came in very handy for this trip.

Thirty minutes later, Evelyn had showered and dressed and was ready to have a one on one with Claude. She would torture him if need be, to get the answers that she needed. She checked her phone one more time to see if Anthony had responded to her text. Still nothing. She wondered what happened to him. She would wait until after her interrogation with Claude then she would give him a call.

She left her room and casually let herself into Claude's room. She gasped. The room was empty... no Claude, no bags, no nothing. It was as if he had disappeared into thin air. The room was perfectly cleaned, but she didn't remember hearing the maids or anyone next door.

She searched the room, the bathroom, there were clean towels, and the sink and tub were dry. No one had taken a shower. Where the hell had he gone?

What the hell was going on?

BOOK II

CHAPTER 17

Two days later, Camille walked into Richard Elia's office. He was standing at the window and seemed to be staring out into the street below.

"Ahem," she said, clearing her throat to get Richard's attention.

"Camille," Richard said as he spun around almost knocking over a vase that was on the shelf next to the window. "I didn't see you standing there."

"Sorry for startling you. The door was open, so I figured I would just come in and let you know that I was back from vacation."

"Please tell me Evelyn came back with you," Richard said.

"She didn't; I left her back at the hotel in St. Thomas," Camille said.

"Are you kidding me?"

"She's a grown woman, Richard, and she can take care of herself. Plus, I'm not her babysitter."

Deep down inside Camille did feel a little guilty leaving her friend back in the islands by herself; after all, this was supposed to be a girl's trip.

"She's a loose cannon," Richard said.

"She'll be alright. She met a guy, and I know that he will take good care of her," She said.

"What guy?" Richard asks.

"His name is Anthony. I don't know him that well, but I don't think that he will do anything to hurt her."

"And you know this how?" Richard asked.

"I know this because I met him, and he has no reason to hurt Evelyn or hurt me for that matter."

This information made Richard uneasy. Evelyn was alone in a country where she didn't know anyone. He wondered why she had to be so goddamned stubborn.

"I need to tell you something Camille, I hired someone to follow you guys in St. Thomas."

"What? Are you crazy? Now she is never going to trust you again. Why would you do something like that?" Camille asked.

"I know, I know. But I had to make sure that everything would be alright with you two," Richard said.

"Does she know?" Camille asked.

"Yeah, somehow she found out and called; and man, was she pissed. But I haven't heard from my guy in days. I fear he might be still there."

"That was not a smart move, Richard. Where did you meet him anyway?"

"I met him at a bar a couple of months ago," He said.

"Is he at least reliable?" she asked.

"Well, I tried digging into his background, and I couldn't find anything. It's like he appeared out of thin air."

Camille sighed, "Well, I tried calling her at the hotel and tried texting too, but she's not responding to my calls or my texts." She mumbled under her breath, "That's not like her."

"I know she probably hates me right now, but I had to do this for her safety. I looked into her background when she first came to work as a profiler," Richard said.

"Well, isn't that your job?"

"Yes, but I had to make sure that she would be the best candidate."

"I know you care about her, but hiring someone to follow us to the Caribbean? That wasn't a good idea," Camille said.

Richard gestured for her to sit in the chair across from his desk and he took a seat in his chair across from her. He took a sip of his coffee and leaned back into his chair.

"The first time I met Evelyn, I fell in love with her instantly Camille, she was beautiful, smart, tough and everything about her just drew me in, I don't know what it was."

He paused for a moment then Camille just looked on and listened without saying anything.

Richard continued, "Evelyn is very intuitive and a brilliant profiler, but she has a temper, and I knew that had to come from someplace. She has a troubled past Camille, and I can feel it."

"I know, she told me when we were having breakfast in the islands."

"So, you knew that she was married before?"

"I do now," Camille said.

"Did she say what happened, what happened to her husband I mean?" Richard asked.

Camille had to make sure that she didn't say too much about what Evelyn had told her. "She didn't really say much, just that he died, and she had to move back home to take care of her mom. Didn't you find anything about her past in your investigations?"

"Not much, that's why I hired Claude to find out as much as he could about her. You don't think he did something to Evelyn, do you?"

Camille waved her hand, "No, nothing like that, you don't need to worry about her."

"When is she supposed to come back home anyway?"

"A week or two, I don't know. She didn't really say. What happened between you and her? Why does she dislike you so much? I thought you two were doing well. She seemed so content when you guys were together."

"Honestly, Camille, I don't know. I thought we were doing well, too. We went out to eat one night, after that we went back to her apartment and we had sex; then I started to tell her that I loved her and I think we should move in together, you know, take the relationship to a more serious level. I think I freaked her out because all I know is the next day, she tells me it's over between us, and then she quits her job that same week. I tried to call her, but she barely answers my calls. I just want to know what I did wrong."

"You guys didn't have an argument or anything?"

"No, she told me she would think about it. Then next thing I know it's over, and now I'm the bad guy," Richard sighed.

"That doesn't sound like the Evelyn I know at all, you sure you didn't say anything else to upset her?" Camille asked.

"Listen, I don't know what is going on with her, and I don't know why she's acting the way that she is. If she doesn't want to be with me, fine, but I need to know that she is alright; that's the only thing that concerns me right now."

"I understand Richard, but maybe she needs time for herself right now, don't push her she will come around. She said she would think about it; maybe this is her time to think."

"I really wished you believed that Camille."

"After all that she has been through, maybe she needs this. Just give her some space and see what happens."

"I'm thinking about going down to St. Thomas if I don't hear from her or Claude soon," Richard said.

"Do you really think that's a good idea?" Camille asked.

"Well, I'm not going to just sit back and let anything bad happen to her."

"Okay, look, Richard. I like you, and I think that you are the best thing that happened to Evelyn. So give me a few days... let me try and get in contact with her again, and then if I don't hear anything back, I will make the trip myself."

"Well, let's make sure that you do hear from her."

Camille eyed him suspiciously.

"You think she suspects anything?" Richard asked, leaning forward in his chair towards Camille.

"No, she doesn't know anything about us."

"Good," Richard said.

Camille didn't like to keep secrets from her best friend Evelyn, but she had to if she wanted to keep her job, and she loved her job.

"How's the family?" Richard asked, jolting her out of her thoughts.

"Everybody is doing just fine, thanks for asking."

"So, when will you be back to work?" Richard asked.

"I'm not sure Rich. Might be next week."

"Good."

Camille got up and walked around the chair towards the door of Richard's office then stopped in the doorway.

"Are we done here; there's somewhere I need to be."

"Camille," Richard looked up at her. "I need you back on this case. You are the best undercover FBI agent that I have."

Camille nodded without turning; she knew exactly what he meant. "Have a good day, sir," she said, then left Richard's office.

CHAPTER 18

Evelyn packed her bags, checked out of the hotel on St. Thomas, and caught the 10 a.m. ferry to the island to meet up with Anthony. But before leaving the area, she stopped at a local jewelry store across the street from the hotel to buy him a beautiful designer watch.

She was smiling now.

She didn't care about Claude anymore, she wasn't thinking about Richard either, she was thinking about her safe place, and that was with Anthony. She really liked him, he was easy to talk to, he didn't judge her, and he didn't expect too much; he just liked her for who she was. It had been a long time since she smiled like that; her face actually felt weird. Was this the feeling of happiness, she wondered to herself?

She wasn't sure, but it sure felt good. She couldn't remember the last time that she was this happy.

She felt her phone vibrate in her shoulder bag, and

when she took it out and noticed that it was a message from Camille, her smile widened.

Hey honey, I'm just checking in
Call me back when you get a chance,
and please be careful. Love you!

Immediately following, a message came through from Richard. The smile quickly faded. "Crap! What now?" she mumbled.

I'm worried about you. Please call me.

Without replying to either text, Evelyn closed the phone and shoved it back into her shoulder bag. She figured that Camille must have seen Richard or told him that she didn't come back home with her. She won't allow Richard's antics to get in the way of this high that she was currently on. No, not this time. After getting to the Island, she rented a car so that she could surprise Anthony. She drove around first trying to follow the familiar places and buildings that she remembered when she was there last, and when Anthony took them around the island. She did remember the restaurant where she and Camille had breakfast the last time they were here.

Her first stop would be at the restaurant to get something to eat because she was now hungry. The next stop would be to find a hotel for her to spend a couple of nights, as she had planned to spend the rest of her visit hopefully with Anthony at his apartment.

The next thing she needed to get after her lunch was a local chip for her phone so that she could text and make calls; her US phone didn't seem to work on the island unless she had Wi-Fi service. When she got close to where the restaurant was located in the town area, it was busy, but by some miracle, she was able to find a parking space that someone was pulling out of across the street in a nearby parking lot. She parked then looked down at her watch. It was 12:30 p.m., lunchtime.

She didn't have to walk far when she saw a sign ahead of her that read "*Caribbean Mobile.*" Perfect. She would get the chip for her cell phone then grab a quick bite, call Anthony and then get a hotel. She liked being here on the island; everything you would need was in walking distance. The mobile store, the banks, restaurant, etc. "How convenient," she thought to herself as she walked out of the mobile store and headed across the street in the direction of the restaurant.

What she saw next made her stop in her tracks. A woman and a man looked like they were arguing in front of the restaurant. When she got closer, she recognized them. "Anthony?" she whispered under her breath.

Now she was even more concerned. She walked closer more slowly, trying to hear the conversation, but Anthony turned, got into his jeep and drove off, leaving the woman outside, whom Evelyn now realized was the chef. But why would they be arguing? This did not look like a bad food order argument, this was something else, and she had to get to the bottom of things. The profiler in her kicked in at this point. The chef was still standing outside, and she was now looking at her cell phone.

Evelyn approached her, "Hey, is everything alright?"

"Oh, hey. Evelyn, right?" the chef asked. The woman was distraught and tried to wipe a single tear with her apron. "Yeah, I'm good now. How are you doing?"

"I am doing well. I just arrived today and wanted to spend some time on the Island, so you might be seeing more of me here. I love this place, especially the food here."

The chef smiled, "Thank you so much. Come on, let us go inside and get you something to eat. You should try today's chef's special, it's great." They both laughed.

When Evelyn got her food, she took out her phone, replaced the new chip, and sent a text to Anthony; it only took him a couple of seconds to reply.

After Evelyn ate her lunch, Julie, the chef, came back to her table and sat down next Evelyn.

"So, how was lunch?" Julie asked.

"It was delish, my compliments to the chef," Evelyn replied.

"I'll be sure to pass on the message," She said.

Evelyn didn't want to pry, but she had to know what was going on with the chef and Anthony, but she had to tread lightly.

"So, chef,"

"Please call me Julie."

"Oh, right... Julie. What was happening earlier? I kind of noticed that you were a little upset; is everything okay? Is there anything I can do to help?"

"Oh, no. It's just a family issue. That's all; nothing to worry about really."

"I just love your accent, where are you from?" She asked her.

"I'm from St. Lucia. I came here about five years ago with my boyfriend and got a job in this restaurant."

"Your boyfriend must be a very lucky guy, huh? He gets to have a live-in chef like you? What a life," Evelyn joked.

"Girl, you are too funny, but it's not like that. Most of the time, he cooks. So at least I get a little break when I get home from the Restaurant," Julie said.

"Oh, my God! The perfect couple." They both laughed.

"Didn't you have a friend with you the last time you were here?"

"Yes, my girlfriend, Camille. She had a family emergency back home, so she had to leave. So now it's just me," she said.

"Well, I have to get back into the kitchen, but it was nice to see you again, Evelyn. Take care of yourself."

When Evelyn had purchased the chip for her cell phone, she got fifty dollars in minutes and 2gb of data, so she was able to search online and find a hotel and book it. She found one that was about ten minutes' drive from her location, and she booked three nights stay just in case. She hadn't planned on staying more than a week then she would head back over to St. Thomas to catch her flight back to the US.

Evelyn paid the bill then walked from the restaurant

to her car, and followed the directions on the phone to the hotel. She wanted to take a little nap and a shower before she met up with Anthony later on. They were going to have dinner and go to a club and hopefully come back to the hotel and spend the night.

Anthony arrived around 7:30 p.m., but they never made it out of the hotel room. When he saw Evelyn, he lifted her into his arms and kissed her passionately. Minutes later, they were in bed, and their clothes were all over the room.

"Hey, beautiful," He said, leaning over her and kissing her on the cheek. "I've missed you so much; I was wondering when you would make it back to see me."

She turned and raised herself up on her elbow and looked at him. "I saw you today. You were talking or arguing with the chef at the restaurant that Camille and I went to the first time we were here. Who is she?"

"I don't want to talk about her right now, I just want to spend this time with you ok," Anthony said.

"Okay, but why were you arguing with her?"

"We were not arguing. We were having a discussion."

"A heated discussion?" she asked him.

"You are so beautiful. You know that I wish I could stay here in this moment a little longer with you." He leaned in and kissed her again.

"Why do you keep changing the subject. Who is Julie to you?"

Evelyn froze when he said, "she's my fiancé."

CHAPTER 19

CLAUDE FINALLY CALLED RICHARD.

"Why the hell did you take so long to get back to me, I was worried that something must have happened?" Richard growled into the phone

"I was doing what you told me to do, I followed them to the hotel, and I was trying to lay low, but I think one of them noticed me, I can't be sure though," Claude said.

"What? How did you let that happen?"

"She is smarter than you think."

"I know she is," Richard interrupted, "And that is why I hired you to keep an eye on her. You were supposed to be smart and stay as far away from her as possible. Just don't do anything else, I will think of something."

"So, you want me to stop following her now? You paid me to do a job, and I will do it until you pay me the rest of my money or until she is on a plane back home."

"Look, I will wire the rest of the money to your

account, just leave her alone. I don't want you to do anything else. Don't follow her, don't approach her, just pack your bags and leave," Richard said over the phone.

Claude smiled to himself. He wondered what had happened to make Richard change his mind about following Evelyn and Camille.

He was curious.

"What happened? Why don't you want me to follow her? I mean them?" Claude asked.

"The plan just changed ok, so don't worry about it, just make sure she doesn't see you again and get the hell out of there."

"Is that right, Richard?" The phone went silent. The employer didn't say another word. Well, I'm doing what you paid me to do, Richard, you paid me to follow your girls, and that is exactly what I am going to do."

"Listen, here, buddy. Evelyn called me. Do you even know that?"

"What the hell are you talking about?"

"When you were passed out drunk, she took your cell phone and called me," Richard said. "I need you to pack your things and get out of there right now."

"I'm not leaving until I finish what I came here to do."

"Who the hell do you think you are?" Richard shouted over the cell phone.

The man laughed, "You can call me Claude, the man you paid to follow Evelyn and Camille," He said with a bit of sarcasm.

"Wait a minute, what kind of game are you playing here?" Richard asked.

"I'm not playing any games, how would it look if I were to walk right up to Evelyn right now and tell her what you, sorry I mean we, have been up to? Do you think that she would ever forgive you?"

There was a long pause on the line. "Ok, what do you want?" the employer asked calmly.

"I want double what you owe me. Wait... make that triple."

"You know I can't do that," Richard said. "I don't have that kind of cash available."

"Yeah, you do," Claude quickly interrupted, "In fact, you have a whole lot more, but I don't want to be greedy."

"When?" he asked after another long pause.

"Let's see, tomorrow, I want to see it in my account tomorrow."

"I can't get you that amount of money by tomorrow, the banks will get suspicious, you know I will get into a lot of trouble."

"I know you're smart Richard, you can find a way; and in the meantime, I'll keep a little eye on Miss Evelyn, you know, so that she doesn't get into trouble, again."

"What do you mean again, what happened to Evelyn, is she alright?"

"Oh, don't worry about Evelyn, she's a tough girl. She just got into a small altercation with a guy who was being kind of fresh, and she took care of it; well, that is, I took care of it for her...and Evelyn won't be seeing or hearing from the man again. See, that's why you paid me to take care of your girl; now you have to take care of me, or else."

"Did you kill him?" Richard asked, concerned.

"Don't worry yourself about that, he's, what you say, sleeping with the fishes," the man laughed at that little joke. The employer did not share in his joke. He was upset, but he tried not to let it be heard in his voice.

"Did you kill him?" he asked again

"The only thing you need to be worried about is getting my money to me."

"Fine, I will get you your money. But if you hurt those women, I swear I will find you and-"

"Don't make promises you can't keep, Richard."

Claude hung up the phone with his employer and smiled to himself. Now, he had to decide which one of the two women he was going to kill first.

CHAPTER 20

"What do you mean she is your fiancé? You never told me you had a fiancé, Anthony. Are you playing games with me?" Evelyn said. She rolled out of bed and started to get dressed; then he stopped her.

"Wait, let me explain," He begged.

"Explain? Are you kidding me, what's there to explain? Are you going to tell me now that you had to stay for the baby?" she asked.

"I'm so sorry that I lied to you, but please, I'm begging you, just have a seat and let me tell you the truth, ok."

It would have been easier for her to let him leave if his accent wasn't so damn sexy and if he wasn't looking all buff sitting there naked on the bed. She caved a little, not because she had fallen for him, but because she was curious to know what kind of explanation he had.

"I'm listening, help me understand why you're here with me when you have a fiancé at home?" she did air quotes with her fingers when she said the word fiancé.

"Julie and I were having problems for years, and I was going to leave her last year, but she told me if I left her she was going to take all my money and go to the police and tell them that I have been abusive to her. So instead of ending things, she gave me her grandmother's ring and told me we would be engaged. But we both knew it wasn't real. I don't love her; I'm just tired of fighting her. She's evil, and she lies just to get attention, telling my friends that I have women all over the country. But then, when I met you, things changed." He touched her chin and smoothed her face with his fingers.

"Are you telling me the truth?" she asked him.

"I wouldn't lie to you." He took her hand and gently kissed it, "I know we just met, but I can't stop thinking about you; every day and night I dream of touching you, holding you again. But I think she may suspect something."

"Why do you say that?"

"One night, I came out of the shower, and she was upset and asked me who Rose was. I must have called your name in my sleep or something because I didn't know why she would ask me that out of the blue. But I told her that you were my coworker."

Evelyn thought about the situation for a bit. The last thing she wanted to do was to be the cause of a relationship ending. Her last relationship had ended because of suspicions of infidelity. But she liked being with Anthony and enjoyed being in his company, and she wasn't looking for a 'relationship'; she just wanted to have some fun if it meant only for a little while.

She sighed.

"I really like you, my sweet Rose. I really don't want what we have to end over this. Please forgive me," Anthony said.

"Don't call me that. Listen, I need to think about this. I'm not here for a relationship, I just wanted to have some fun, but I'm not going to ruin a relationship." She began to rise when Anthony gently pulled her towards him and kissed her lips gently.

She wanted to pull away from his lips, but they were so soft and sensual, and she melted. His touch was gentle. He was gentle; even more now than they had been almost a half-hour ago.

She groaned for him to stop, but she didn't want him to stop; every hair on her body stood on end in pleasure. And then she was lost in Anthony. She had forgotten about his fiancé, she had forgotten about Richard, and she had forgotten about Claude. If only she could bury herself in him and never leave, never see Richard again, and never go back home to the states.

After they were done making love, Anthony held her close to him and kissed her gently on her cheeks.

"Are you ok, my sweet Rose?" He asked her.

"Yeah, I'm fine. I'm here with you," She lied. She could hear Camille's voice now, 'I told you, you don't know him, you can't trust him.' And she knew her friend was right; as a matter of fact, she was always right; and now she wished that she was still here on vacation with her. She made a mental note to call her in the morning. She missed her friend's voice. What was she thinking spending the night with a man she barely knew? She didn't know. She had always done this. She would rush into things — into relationships — and then regret it afterward. When will she ever learn? But it was a good thing she wasn't in so deep with this man. She hadn't fallen in love with him yet, or had she? "Oh my God!" she thought to herself. Had she fallen for Anthony?

No. The situation was beginning to feel terrifying and wonderful at the same time. Which made it all confusing, and she didn't like being confused. Her head was starting to hurt. She was doing a lot of thinking, that was not like her at all. This man had done something to Evelyn; he had tamed her and bought her to her knees.

She was so into her thoughts that she didn't realize that he had gone quiet, and his breathing had slowly changed to snoring. It wasn't loud; it was soft and steady and perfect. Everything about this man seemed perfect. But he wasn't, he was just a man, just like every other man. He had lied to her.

Evelyn eased quietly out of bed, making sure not to wake Anthony, and slipped on a shirt and underwear. Reaching into her bag, she grabbed her cell phone. There were messages from Camille and her mom, but surprisingly there were none from Richard. She read the couple that were from Camille and responded by telling her that she was okay and would be home soon. She closed the phone and sat in the chair by the bed and watched as Anthony slept.

The FBI profiler in her kicked in at this point as she thought about what Anthony had told her about Julie giving him her grandmother's ring. She knew a liar when she saw one, and Anthony was a sweet guy, a loving, caring guy, but he was hiding something. She didn't buy it. What he didn't know was that she had met Julie, and the woman didn't have any reason to lie to Evelyn. She didn't know who she was... or that she was seeing Anthony. He wasn't lying when he said that she had suspected that he was seeing someone else. But that was the only thing that was true.

Anthony was like any other man that she had met before; they wanted to have their cake and eat it too.

"You ok?" she heard Anthony say as he yawned. "I'm fine, just have a lot on my mind right now," Evelyn replied.

"What time is it?" he said, glancing at his watch.

Evelyn shrugged. She watched him as he leaned out of bed and reached for his boxers, then his jeans and put them on. Then he grabbed his shirt. She didn't say anything.

"Will I see you tomorrow?" he asked as he walked over to her and kissed her forehead.

"Mhm." She nodded and smiled.

"My sweet Rose," He said, leaving the room and closing the door behind him.

CHAPTER 21

Evelyn knew that getting involved with Anthony was a big no, a huge mistake; it might be a risk too. Did she really believe in love at first sight, did it even exist?

When he left, Evelyn had showered, trying to wash off his scent and any memory that lingered on her body. She then changed into her pajamas and grabbed a bottle of wine that she had purchased earlier before she checked into the hotel and poured herself a glass. She was alone again; Camille had gone back home to her family, and she had no one. Why had she come here? She thought to herself. The strange thing about the night was not only that she was alone, but that she was alone in a strange country and everything was unfamiliar to her; the sounds, the neighbors arguing down the street, the music playing from a nearby bar; even the dogs bark differently in the islands.

Tonight, it was just Evelyn and an empty hotel room

on a vacation that was supposed to be spent with her and Camille.

She moved slowly from the chair where she was sitting and sipping on her wine to the door that looked like a window that led to a small porch at the back of the hotel room. She never quite noticed that porch there before. There were two chairs, she sat in one and looked out at the night sky. It had been a while since she had looked up at the stars and the moon, the sky was so black and blue. Why did everything seem so different and so beautiful in this part of the world, but still so confusing?

The night was cool, the trees swayed a little, but not too much in the gentle breeze. She inhaled the fresh, crisp air. What was that smell? Someone was cooking something. She didn't recognize the aroma, but it smelled delicious. She wasn't the best cook, and somehow, she thought that might have partly been the reason why her marriage didn't work. No, her ex-husband had been a terrible man; he was controlling, and everything had to be his way or no way. Everything had to be perfect; that was the reason.

A dog started to bark in the distance and broke her thoughts; then another dog started, then another. Evelyn felt alone again; it was a feeling that was unfamiliar to her. She had her job, which kept her busy most of the time, then she had Camille, then Richard. There was no reason for her to feel alone.

She took another sip of her wine and looked back up at the starry sky. What was it about her and relationships? Why didn't they seem to work or last? What was it about her that was afraid of commitment?

She thought about Anthony for a moment and considered that maybe a relationship between them might work after all. She lived in the United States, and he lived here in the islands, they wouldn't have to commit to each other. She had the money so she could travel once a month to see him, they would have great sex then she would go back to the states, no string attached. But what was it about the whole situation that made her feel so guilty?

She sipped on her wine glass again then realized that it was empty. She also realized that it was too late to get anything to eat, every place had already closed.

Evelyn went back inside and poured another glass of wine and noticed that the light on her phone was blinking; checking the phone, it was a text from Camille. She had been worried about Evelyn and had not heard from her in days. She looked at the date on the message. She texted five minutes ago. "What was she doing up at this hour?"

She dialed the number and Camille picked up on the second ring.

"Camille?" Evelyn asked.

"Evelyn, are you alright? I have been calling and texting you. You had me so worried I almost had to take another trip back to St. Thomas."

"I'm okay, Cam. What are you doing up at this hour?"

"I had to use the bathroom, and I figured I would try and text you one last time before I went back to bed."

"I came to see Anthony," She sighed.

"Wow, okay. Well, you don't seem happy about that. What happened?"

"Well, I found out tonight that he has a fiancé."

"Are you kidding me? I knew there was something up with that guy. Girl, I'm sorry, I could tell that you really liked him too. Where are you staying now?"

"I'm at a hotel; it's not the best like the one on St. Thomas. but at least it's clean," Evelyn said.

"When are you coming back home, Ev?" Camille asked her.

"Soon. Actually, sooner than I had expected. I can't believe I was so stupid, Camille."

"Don't beat yourself up Ev, it happens sometimes, everybody makes mistakes. But he was such a nice guy; I can't believe he didn't tell you that he has a girl. What did you do when you found out?"

"Ummm..."

"Eeeeev... what did you do?" Camille said.

"I had sex with him."

"Evelyn Rose Dubois! No, you didn't!"

"I know, I know, but he was so damned irresistible. And I felt a little sorry for him, plus, did I say he was irresistible?"

"I can't with you right now; you need to hurry up and come home. Have you spoken to Richard?"

"He texted me, but I didn't respond," Evelyn said.

"Okay," Camille said. She didn't want to upset Evelyn by talking about Richard anymore.

"I think I'm getting a headache now. I need to get some rest, okay? I will talk to you tomorrow."

"Okay, I love you, sweetie. Just be careful, ok?" They both hung up.

Evelyn bit down on her lower lip. Her mind flashed back to just hours ago when she and Anthony were wrapped up in each other's arms, and he whispered sweetness into her ears. What was it about him that made her weak? What was it about him that made her yearn for him? This was wrong; this was so wrong. But he wasn't married, at least not yet.

She had finished the bottle of wine and slowly crept over to the side of the bed. The room seemed to be spinning now, and the walls felt to be closing in, and all at once, the room was getting smaller. What was happening? Her heart began to pound heavily in her ears, her throat felt tight, her breathing had become rapid, and she was starting to feel dizzy. Was she having a heart attack?

No.

Evelyn was having a panic attack. She recognized the symptoms. The symptoms that she had before, many years ago. When she was married to her husband/ex-husband. She could hardly keep her eyes open now, they were getting heavy, and she was getting weak. What was happening? Her vision had become blurred but not so much that she didn't make out the dark figure that opened the door and stepped into the room.

"Hello? Who are you, what do you want?" the words

got caught in her throat, but the figure didn't say anything, just moved slowly towards her.

"Get out! Get out right now!" she yelled, but it barely came out above a whisper. "No," she said, and then suddenly the vision of her husband coming towards her with the knife came clearly into focus.

"No! It can't be. Stop! Please don't hurt me!"

When the figure came closer to the bed, they stood over her, and she noticed that something was covering the head. A hat? A hoodie?

She recognized the intruder at once, or did she?

"Julie?" she said. Then everything went black.

CHAPTER 22

It was 8:30 the next morning when Evelyn woke up with a splitting headache and an empty wine bottle on the floor. Her head was pounding and reeling at the same time. Had she gotten drunk? Evelyn rolled over to the side of the bed, and picked up the empty bottle from the floor, threw it in the trash can and headed into the bathroom. She tried to remember what had taken place on the previous night. Sex with Anthony, and thinking about it now, she knew it was a mistake. Having sex with a man who was on his way down the aisle was never a good idea. Having sex with anyone who was attached is never a good idea.

As a teenager, she remembered almost coming to blows with a classmate because she had kissed her boyfriend. She didn't know that they were still an item at the time because the boy had told her that he had broken up with his girlfriend. That was a hard lesson to learn at an early age. Evelyn didn't know how to fight back then, and she was not going to stand around and have a girl beat her up in front of the whole school.

How was this different from then?

She had met a guy. He eventually told her the truth, but who was going to stop his fiancé from beating her ass when she found out?

Evelyn was out of her element. No one was going to stand up for her if she got into trouble. It would be her word against Anthony's fiancé. She could hear Camille's voice in her head already, "Evelyn, you don't know anything about this guy." She was right, of course; she had only spent a couple of days with him. What did she really know about him?

A knock at the door rattled her out of her thoughts, and she jumped a little. She quickly washed her face and wiped it with the towel that hung on a rack next to her. She looked in the mirror one last time and brushed back a few stray strands of hair with her fingers.

The knocks came again even louder this time, and she quickly walked to the door and opened it.

"Good morning Beautiful," Anthony said as he leaned in and kissed her cheek.

"Hey," Evelyn said.

"Did I wake you?"

"No, I was in the bathroom."

"I bought you breakfast, I thought you might be hungry," Anthony said, handing her a bag and a bottle of orange juice.

"Thanks, I'm starving," She replied, taking the bag and putting it on a small table next to the bed.

"How did you sleep?"

Evelyn thought for a bit and wondered to herself. How did I sleep? Somehow, she could still feel the effects of the past couple of hours, but she wasn't sure what the effects were a result of. She tried hard to remember, but all she could remember was talking to Camille, and emptying the wine bottle, and everything after that was a blur.

"I slept ok," She finally said. "I just have a little headache, but I'll be ok. Let me take a shower then I will be back, ok?"

Evelyn spun around and grabbed her robe and headed back into the bathroom. Five minutes under the warm spray of the shower woke her and removed any blockage of the night before from her brain.

Now she remembered.

The man had come into the hotel, no, wait, it was a woman, she was wearing a black hoodie, and it was pulled down over her eyes. Was it a dream? She shook it off and considered that it must have been the wine together with her imaginations running wild.

She stepped out of the shower and slipped on her robe and brushed her hair back into a ponytail. She entered the room just in time to see Anthony remove his cell phone from his ear. He had taken off his shirt and was leaning against two pillows on the bed, and he smiled when he saw Evelyn enter from the bathroom.

"You look so beautiful, Rose," He said.

"You know, only one other person in the world called me Rose."

"Is that true?" he asked, leaning up and pulling her towards him. "Tell me."

"My very first boyfriend used to call me Black Rose because bad luck seemed to follow me everywhere I went," she laughed a little. The truth was, it wasn't her first boyfriend who called her that, it had been her ex-husband, and he called her that whenever he would beat her and talk down to her. But she couldn't let Anthony in on that part of her life. Not yet, not now.

"You are so beautiful, Rose, I just love to see you smile and I love to hear your voice when you talk." He took her hand and kissed it gently. "I wish I could stay all day with you."

Evelyn took her hand away and got up and walked over to the table where she had placed the bag earlier with the breakfast inside.

"What's wrong?"

She shook her head, "Nothing, I'm just hungry. What did you get us to eat?"

"Sandwiches with scrambled egg and bacon, I wasn't sure what you ate for breakfast."

"This is fine, thanks."

She turned to look at him and found him staring in her direction. God, this man was so handsome and sexy, she just wished that things could be different. Why did he have to come into her life now? Why did he have a fiancé or a girlfriend? She knew that she really needed to end things between them before it got too complicated or at least put some distance there so that he could sort out his life, then maybe they could get back together. It would be much easier if the sex wasn't so amazing. But was that wishful thinking?

"Babe?" Anthony whispered in her ear. She didn't notice that he had gotten up from the bed and slid behind her. He wrapped his arms around her and kissed her ear then her neck. "I missed you so much last night. I couldn't stop thinking about you."

Evelyn knew this was wrong, but it felt so good.

"Hold on a second. I still can't forget the fact that you live with your fiancé, I don't want to come between you two."

"You don't have to worry baby. You are the only person that I want to be with right now; I'm here with you, let's not ruin this okay? I just want to hold you and kiss you and make sweet love to you all day; well, until the next hour when I have to leave and go to work," He said with a smile.

Evelyn took a deep breath and closed her eyes and let Anthony consume all of her, and thirty minutes later, they were both out of breath and lying in each other's arms.

There was another knock at the door. Who was knocking at this hour? No one even knew she was here; let alone in this hotel room. She looked at Anthony, and he looked at her, then the knock came again. She finally swung her legs over the side of the bed and reached for her robe at the foot of the bed and threw it on. She opened the door, and her heart gave a wild thump as she stared at the single black rose in a long-stemmed wine glass.

CHAPTER 23

"Everything ok?" Anthony asked as he got up from the bed and walked over to where Evelyn stood with the door partially open. She then quickly closed it when she saw Anthony approaching, but it was too late for her to hide her surprise or the black rose in her hand. She didn't want to let Anthony in on what was going on with her. She was having too much fun with him and didn't want to ruin it.

But the black rose did that for her.

"What is that?" he said, pointing at the rose in her hand.

"I found it on the carpet outside the door; it's probably a mistake."

Anthony chuckled. "Is that from your ex?"

Evelyn froze and stared at Anthony. "Wh-what? Why would you say that?"

"Remember you told me the story about your ex

calling you a black rose, I just saw the rose and thought about the story, that was so funny."

Evelyn forced a fake laugh and dumped the rose and the vase in the nearby trash can. But she was quick to slip the note that was attached to it into her pocket before Anthony saw it. She would read it later, but she was pretty sure she knew what was written on it.

"I guess it was kind of funny." She said, but she didn't think that it was funny at all.

Anthony looked at his watch and kissed Evelyn on the cheek. "Sorry babe but I have to go now. I have a couple of errands to run before work. Will I see you later?"

Evelyn shrugged, "Sure," she said.

She watched him get dressed and leave. She then dug into her pocket and retrieved the small envelope and pulled out the note inside.

Her mouth dropped open as she stared at the note in her hand and let it slip from her grasp slowly unto the floor. She had to think. Then she picked up the phone and placed a call to Camille, and as usual, she answered on the second ring.

"Hello, this is Camille." She said,

"It's me," Evelyn said.

"Hey hun, what's wrong?" Camille asked, now concerned because she could hear the distress in Evelyn's voice, and instantly knowing that something was up.

"I'm-" she paused, then continued, "why aren't you at work today?"

"Maya came down with a fever today, so I had to stay home and take care of her. What's up with you today? I can hear something strange in your voice."

"Oh, my poor baby."

"She will be alright. What's up with you?"

"Well I have to tell you something, you're not going to like it, but I need your advice. I don't know what to do."

"Is it about Anthony?" Camille asked.

"No, no, it's not about Anthony."

"Okay... well, then tell me."

Evelyn took a deep breath and paused a bit before saying anything.

"You remember the black rose that I got at the hotel in St. Thomas?"

"Umm.... Yes, I remember it had a note attached to it as well, what about it?"

"I got another one this morning at my hotel room, and I don't know why or what to do."

"Are you freaking kidding me?" Camille yelled into the phone.

"And there was another note attached too," Evelyn continued ignoring her friend.

"I'm booking the next flight for you out of there, and you better make sure that you're on it or I will come and get you and drag you here myself."

"Wait, I think I need to find out who is sending me these roses."

Camille tried to calm herself down before she asked the question. "Well, what did the note say?"

"It has numbers on it, well it looks like a date, but the date didn't make any sense to me.

"What was the date, Evelyn?"

She called her Evelyn; Camille didn't call her full name unless she was upset.

"As I said, I don't know what it means, but I really think I should find out, give me a day or two and if I don't get anywhere, I will catch the very next plane back to the city, I promise."

"Fine, but I'm calling Richard as soon as I hang up from you."

"No, please I don't want to get him involved in this, just give me some time, ok?

"Ok, two days then I'm calling the airline. Look, call me later so I can know that you're ok. I don't feel comfortable having you there by yourself. You need to be here. So, do what you need to do, and please come home in one piece Ev. I'm getting scared for you now. Please take care of yourself."

"I will, babe. You know I can take care of myself. Don't worry; I will be fine."

They both hung up the phone and once again Evelyn had lied to her best friend. The note didn't just have numbers on it; they were very specific numbers. It read:

RIP EVELYN ROSE DUBOIS
01.05.82 – 07.30.19

Evelyn quickly got an idea. She took the note from

the floor along with the vase and the black rose and put them in a plastic bag. It hadn't occurred to her before that she needed to preserve them so that she could get the fingerprints or any DNA evidence from the contents.

Why the heck didn't she think about that before? She could kick herself. She used to be an FBI agent for crying out loud. That should have been the first thing that came to mind. But she got distracted, but what was distracting her? Anthony.

She wrapped them up carefully and put the contents into her suitcase, she would have them tested when she got back to the US in a couple of days, but for now, she wondered where she was going to start?

She quickly cleaned up the room as best she could, picked up her shoulder bag, and headed to the door. The knock at the door startled her and stopped her in her tracks.

"Who is it now?" she whispered to herself. She looked around quickly to see what she could find just in case she needed to defend herself. She grabbed the empty bottled from the nearby trash can and held it behind her back as she edged closer to the door. Her heart raced a little, and she could hear the thump, thump of her beating heart in her ears.

She closed her eyes and inhaled deeply and gathered what little courage she had, then opened her eyes again. There was the knock again. She didn't want to lose them this time, so she grabbed the door and pulled it open with all her strength.

She froze.

The words took their time getting from her brain to her lips. Then when she finally opened her mouth, even her own voice was strange to her.

"What are you doing here?"

CHAPTER 24

Two hours later, after speaking with Evelyn, Camille stormed into Richard's office of the FBI building without knocking or making an appointment. Richard was on the phone and waved his hand for her to close the door and have a seat, which she did.

"What's up, I thought you weren't coming in today?" Richard asked.

"I need you to call Evelyn today and tell her what you did."

"I've tried calling her; she doesn't want to talk to me. She's a grown woman, Camille, and I won't force her."

"I need you to talk to her and tell her to come home. I can't take this anymore; if anything happens to her in that place, I won't be able to forgive myself."

"Hold on, what's going on?" Richard asked.

"She's in trouble," Camille said.

"What?"

"Wait, let me explain. Evelyn and I were in St.

Thomas when we received a package, and it was a dozen roses - Black roses."

Richard furrowed his eyebrows seemingly confused, but he waited for Camille to finish.

"And there was a note in the package as well. The note read *'RIP EVELYN ROSE DUBOIS.'* Now, I thought it was strange and Evelyn told me it was a mistake --that someone must have played a prank. Evelyn called me this morning, and I could hear the fear in her voice. I think she is very scared now."

"Are you kidding me, Camille? Do you know what that means? That is a death threat, and you left her there in that country alone? I really don't know what has gotten into you two these days."

"Hold on Rich. She told me she changed hotels and she is still getting the black roses and the notes."

Richard tried to stay calm, but he was furious now. He rubbed his head and looked at Camille.

"I gave you one thing to do, keep an eye on Evelyn and see to it that she doesn't get into any trouble, and now this. I swear, if anything happens to that girl, it is all on you."

"Oh no, you don't. You will not put the blame on me, Richard. If you ask me, this whole thing is out of control because of you and your actions. You just couldn't leave well enough alone. You had to be the controlling boyfriend. Evelyn is a grown woman; she is not a puppet on a string, and she is not going to sit and do what you want when you want just because you say so."

Camille rarely ever lost her temper, but this whole situation was about to become a ticking time bomb.

"What are you talking about?" Richard said, interrupting her.

"I wasn't the one who hired a psycho to follow us not knowing who this guy is and what he is capable of. Are you kidding me?"

"He's not a psycho?"

"Really?" Camille stood up and folded her arms. "And where exactly did you find this guy."

"It doesn't matter where I found him or met him right now. I'm sorry ok, will you sit down so I can talk to you. Please."

Camille sat back down in the chair opposite of Richard and unfolded her arms.

"What else did Evelyn say?" Richard continued.

"She didn't say much else, but I'm pretty sure that she wants to solve this, I mean to find out who has been leaving the roses. She's in over her head, Rich. You need to call her and get her the hell out of there today, or your girlfriend will be dead by tomorrow Rich!"

"Ex-Girlfriend," he said.

"Are you going to call her or not? I don't have time to go back and forth with you."

"I'll call her, don't worry about it. We will get her back here in one piece."

"I hope so."

"If I have to go down there myself and get her, we are going to get her back here. But I need you to do something for me."

"What's that?"

"Use your skills and your resources and see if you can locate Claude. I can give you the number he used while in St. Thomas, but I'm not sure if he will still answer it. If we can get his exact location, then maybe we can figure out if he is in the same location as Evelyn and then work from there. And I also want to know Evelyn's every movement from today onwards. I need you to track her phone as well."

"It's like we're right back where we started, following Evelyn without her knowledge," Camille shook her head.

"The only difference is we are trying to save her life; it's the only way, Camille," Richard reassured her.

"If you say so," Camille said as she stood up to leave.

"Camille, don't let this get to you. I'm confident that Evelyn can take care of herself; he can't get rid of her that easily. But I need you to get your head in the game."

"I have to leave now; I left my daughter at my mother's, and she has to go out in a few minutes. I'll give you an update on whatever I find as soon as I find it."

"Thanks," Richard said.

CHAPTER 25

"WHAT ARE YOU DOING HERE, JULIE?" EVELYN ASKED as the woman walked past her into the hotel room. "Well, come in, why don't you?" Evelyn threw her hands up and rolled her eyes, closing the door behind her.

"We need to talk," Julie said, sitting in a chair across from Evelyn bed.

"I really don't have time for this. I have some things I need to do. Maybe we can talk later; I'll come by the restaurant."

"No, we need to talk right now. Please have a seat." Julie motioned towards another empty chair across from her.

"Fine," Evelyn said and finally took a seat. Evelyn wasn't a woman who took orders from people she didn't know, but there was something about the way she spoke, it was eerie. It was not the same Julie that she spoke to at the restaurant. No, this was something else. She looked pale and a bit disheveled... like she had not combed her hair today. She noticed the bags under her eyes. Had she not slept in days?

"Wait a minute, how did you know where to find me, I never told you or anybody that I was staying here?" she quickly wished she could swallow those words. Why did she say that? She had no idea what this woman was going to do to her. Had she come here to harm her? Nobody knew she was at this hotel, not Camille, not Richard, not even her mother. 'Good job, Evelyn. She could cut up your body and bury you somewhere, and no one would even know.'

Enough.

"Relax, I'm not here to hurt you," Julie said as she smiled at Evelyn.

'Did she just read my mind?' Evelyn thought to herself. "Did you follow me here?"

"Don't be silly. I followed Anthony last night. I knew that he was up to something and that he was going to see someone, but I never imagined that it would be you. Imagine my surprise when you opened the door."

"I don't understand, why would you follow him?"

"Because I know him, he's a womanizer. You think you're the only woman that he's been with while he was with me. Honey, there were several others. You are just another notch in his belt. He doesn't care about you," Julie laughed. But Evelyn noticed something strange about her laugh; it was evil. Who was this woman?

"You're lying. You would say anything about him just so that you can come between us." Evelyn stood up and walked over to the door, "I think it's time for you to leave now."

"Well honey, I'm not finished saying what I have to say."

"You're finished, so get out of here right now."

"Stay away from my man or else." Julie stood up and faced Evelyn, but Evelyn stood her ground and looked her right in her eye.

"If he's the type of the man that you claim him to be, then why don't you just leave him or let him go? Let him live his own life. He doesn't love you anymore."

"Is that what he's been telling you? He doesn't love me? Well, I've got news for you honey, he's mine, and he belongs to me, and he will always belong to me, and neither you or any other woman out there gon' ever take him away from me." A sly grin passed across Julie's lips.

"Are you saying what I think you're saying? Tell me it isn't so!"

"I don't know what you are speaking of?"

"Have you done something to Anthony?"

They stared at each other, and for a moment, no one said anything. What was going on here? What had she done now, what had she gotten herself into? She knew that this relationship was too good to be true, and she should have followed her guts.

"Were you the one who left the black rose by the door earlier? Are you trying to scare me?"

"What are you talking about?"

"It makes sense now; you are a crazy person."

"Crazy!" Julie glared at Evelyn.

The way that Julie looked at Evelyn, if this had been the movies, her head would have popped off, and green pea soup would have been overflowing from her. This woman was pissed, and Evelyn was amused a little, but she held her composure. She felt that any moment now she was going to burst out laughing. Why was she entertaining this naïve, delusional, crazy woman? She thought to herself. She rolled her eyes.

"Listen I don't have time for this, there's someplace I have to be so if you don't mind leaving."

Evelyn reached for the door and opened it a bit, but out of nowhere, Julie pushed it and slammed it shut. She grabbed Evelyn by the arm and spun her around to face her. Evelyn could feel her hands squeezing tighter and tighter and her fingernails digging into her flesh.

"Let go of me you psycho," Evelyn said and pulled away from her grasp.

"Hear me and hear me good. You are going to stay away from Anthony or else."

"Are you threatening me?"

Julie stepped back when she realized that Evelyn was serious. Not only that, she hadn't noticed that Evelyn had picked up an empty wine bottle and held it firmly in her hand. When and where did she get an empty wine bottle?

"No, you hear me good! I don't like to be threatened, and if I see you anywhere in my vicinity, I'm calling the police, and have you arrested for stalking and threatening me. I don't care about you and your relationship with Anthony because I'm going to be gone in a couple of days and you never have to see me again."

"Just stay away..."

Evelyn interrupted. "I heard you the first time. Now get out, you crazy bat!" she yelled.

Without hesitation, Julie walked to the door and opened it, and without looking back, she left. Evelyn let out a slow, steady breath. Why do bad things seem to follow her wherever she went; maybe her ex-husband was right. Maybe she was a black rose. She dismissed that thought right out of her mind.

Her cell phone buzzed inside her bag, and she quickly took it out and looked at the caller id. She instantly recognized the number; it was Richard. "What now?" she said and put the phone back in her bag. She wasn't ready to have Richard yelling at her like she was a child. She was sure that Camille had told him everything. After all, that was her best friend, and she was only looking out for her. Her phone buzzed again, "Not now Richard, she murmured, but this time it was her mother. She hadn't heard from her in days, and she was concerned. She couldn't deal with her mother at this moment, she didn't have time to answer her questions, but she would be sure to let her in on everything as soon as she got back home. She really did miss her.

When she reached her rental car, she got in and slipped the key into the ignition. She looked up and noticed it; another black rose on her windscreen. She thought for a moment, 'What was the date today?' then she remembered, it was July... the 29th.

CHAPTER 26

"Hi, I'm Special Agent Camille Somble," Camille stated, as she took out her badge, opened it, and turned it face forward toward the young woman at the counter.

"Okay," the young woman raised an eyebrow and stared at her in confusion while she chewed slowly on her gum. The young woman looked like she was in her early twenties, and this was probably her first real job.

"I need some assistance; is there a supervisor I can speak with?" Camille asked her.

"Yeah, Umm, sure. Can you hold on a minute?" the woman said, then disappeared around the corner.

Camille took a seat in the nearby chair and glanced through a magazine that she picked up from a nearby table. Richard told her to check into Evelyn, but she had a better idea. She was going to check the number Richard had given her, Claude's cell phone number. He probably would have turned it off or gotten rid of it by now, but she took a chance.

This was the fourth cell phone company that she had gone to. The others didn't have his number registered with them. Hopefully, this cell phone company had the information that she desperately needed.

"Agent Somble?" the tall man approached her. "Hi, I'm Edward Lee, and I'm the store manager here, how may I help you?"

"Is there somewhere private where we can talk?"

"Sure," the man said and pointed in the direction of his office where she followed him.

"I need your help in tracking a cell phone number, I hope you can help me," she said when he closed the door behind them.

"Yes ma'am, I think I should be able to do that, please have a seat." He motioned toward the chair across from his desk.

They both sat down, and the man turned to his laptop and started to punch the keys. Camille slipped him a piece of paper with the name and cell phone number written on it.

"Can I ask what this is about? We don't usually give out personal information about our clients," Edward said.

"The only thing I can say is I'm looking for a suspect in a case. I don't need a lot of information, I just need his name and address, if there is one. Oh and one more thing, I know that this might be impossible, but would you be able to locate his phone?"

"Okay, well if the GPS is on it shouldn't be difficult to track at all.

"Great, I'd appreciate that so much."

"No problem, anything we can do to help," Edward said. He punched the keys a few more times, and in less than five minutes, he had the information. I have a name and an address. Mr. Claude Amos."

Edward wrote down Claude's name and address and slid the paper over to Camille. She looked at it. He was in Brooklyn, which wasn't that far from there. "And I have located that phone for you also." He said with a smile.

"Oh great, where exactly in the Caribbean is he?"

Edward looked at her, confused, "Oh, no, actually the phone's location is here in the United States. Would you like the address of that location as well?" he asked.

"That would be great, thanks."

Camille took the second piece of paper and put it into her jacket pocket without looking at it. The first thing she wanted to know, who Claude was and why was he after Evelyn?

After they said their goodbyes, Evelyn entered Claude's address into her GPS and drove a couple of miles until she found the place.

She found a parking space up the street and walked the rest of the way, just in case he was home. From the outside, the place looked like a studio, and she had to be buzzed in, in order to get into the building. She pressed a few buttons, making sure not to press Claude's. No one answered the door. She decided to walk along the street to see if there was an alley or a back way that she could get in.

As she was about to leave, the door opened, and an elderly man with a cane and a young woman who looked like a nurse walked out of the door. She smiled at them and nodded and quickly walked past them to grab the door before it closed again. She barely made it.

His unit was on the third floor of the building, and she climbed the stairs, as she didn't want to bump into him, fearing that he would recognize her. She was sure that he knew by now who she was and what she looked like, after all, he was in St. Thomas with her and Evelyn.

When she reached the third floor, she slowly walked to his door. She put her ear to the door and listened.

Nothing.

She then knocked as hard as she could. Still nothing. She took a deep breath and turned the knob; the door was locked. "Dammit," she cursed under her breath.

She looked around the hallway and noticed a rug. Please be a key under it. Please. When she bent down and pulled it, there was a key. She stood up and quietly unlocked the door. There was a click then a low creek then the door opened into an almost dark room that was barely lit by a window that was completely covered by dark-colored curtains.

"Hello? Anyone here?" she said before she stepped in the room and closed the door behind her. No one answered.

She pulled out her cell phone and switched on the flashlight while she searched for a light or a wall switch.

She found a lamp that was next to a desk and switched it on. On the desk were two computer screens. She punched the keyboard a few times, and it came on but had a password prompt. What was she looking for exactly? She searched the drawers and found nothing that would indicate information about her or Evelyn. There were a couple of receipts for equipment and some for takeout restaurant menus.

She looked around the room and saw empty takeout boxes next to a mattress on the floor. She lifted the mattress, nothing.

She continued to search the apartment when her phone buzzed in her jacket pocket and startled her a bit. She took out her phone and noticed it was her mother.

"Mom? Everything okay?" she asked. "Alright, I'm on my way," she said, then replaced the phone back into her pocket. That was when she noticed two doors at the far end of the room, and one door was partially opened. She walked over to the door and slightly pulled it, but it was the bathroom, then she closed it back. The other door was a couple of feet away and completely closed.

She slowly opened the door. The room was small and tight like a closet and empty except for a sheet that was hung against the wall. She stepped inside and found the light switch and pulled it, then pulled the sheet from the wall.

She gasped.

"What the devil?" she whispered.

On the wall were pictures, hundreds of pictures; some of Evelyn, some of her house, some of them with

Evelyn and Richard, some of them with her and Evelyn on St. Thomas. The pictures looked like they had been arranged in order of when they were taken. The earliest pictures were at the top, but the pictures at the bottom were what made Camille's heart felt like it stopped.

She took out her cell phone and placed a call to Richard. The phone rang, but he didn't pick up. "Shit. Shit. Shit! Pick up the phone, Rich!" she screamed softly into the phone. When his voice finally came on, it was his answering service. She hung up and called his office.

"Hello, I need to speak to Richard Alias urgently please, this is Special Agent Camille." She paused when she saw the last picture of Evelyn.

"Hello? Ma'am? Are you still there?" the woman on the line said.

"Hold on," she said, as she pulled the last photo from the wall so she could get a closer look. "I'm sorry, what did you say."

"I was saying that Mr. Alias is in a meeting and he asked not to be disturbed. Do you-"

"Thank you," Camille said before the woman could finish her sentence then hung up the phone.

She held the photo closer to the light. In her hand was a picture of Evelyn laying with her eyes closed, and it looked like she was dead. Her hands were placed neatly over her stomach, and she had what looked like flowers adorning her head like a crown. "Is she lying in a coffin? Oh, my God!" Camille felt the tear roll down her cheek.

This was a picture of Evelyn at her own funeral. In

her hand was a single black rose and above her head in writing the words *R.I.P. Evelyn Rose Dubois.*

Camille put the photo in her pocket. Then she remembered the address Edward had given her. She took it out quickly and looked at it. She recognized the address and quickly left Claude's studio, not forgetting to lock the door and put back the key.

She took the steps two at a time as she sped down the flight of stairs. Hopefully, the picture was a fake, and she could get it analyzed at the office. Evelyn was in more danger than she or Richard had ever imagined.

Was Claude Amos even his real name? At this point, she was pretty sure that it wasn't.

'Evelyn, I hope you're still alive. Please call me,' she said to herself and drove off.

CHAPTER 27

AFTER THE CALL FROM CAMILLE, EVELYN TOOK THE ferry to St. Thomas and booked a suite at the same hotel that she and Camille had stayed at when they first arrived. All the other rooms were completely booked, so she had to get a suite which was a few hundred dollars more, but she didn't care; she just needed a place, a bottle of alcohol, and a bed. She was not a woman to drown her sorrows in tears when alcohol always did the trick.

Camille was frantic when she called her, she was saying that Claude was back in the United States and was planning something big, but she didn't go into much detail before the phone went dead.

After taking a hot shower, she slid into her robe and poured herself a glass of red wine. She needed this after all that she went through the past couple of weeks. She was almost raped, someone was following her, a crazed woman wanted to beat her up, then, the thing with Anthony... It was getting to be too much. Then the black rose at the hotel. But wait, she sat up straight in the chair. If Claude was back in the United States who left the rose by the door and what about the dates? These things were not adding up.

She pulled out her cell phone and dialed Camille, then she stopped, hung up then dialed Richard. There was no answer. She put the phone down and continued to sip on her wine. She was tired. She was tired of everything, tired of thinking, tired of wondering, and she was starting to get a headache. Then, she remembered she hadn't eaten all day.

She called down to the reception and placed an order for room service, where she ordered the smoked salmon dinner, with wild rice and spring green salad. She hung up and tried calling Richard again. There was still no answer. She tried calling his office but didn't get him either. It seemed crazy that all the other times he was dying to talk to her, and now he wasn't picking up. She tried calling Camille, and after the second ring, her answering machine came on.

"What in the world was going on. Why is no one answering the phone," she said. She hoped that nothing had happened to them; she began to worry again. Then she thought to herself it wouldn't be long now. Camille had gotten her a ticket back to the United States for the following morning, so at least she would be going home.

Fifteen minutes later, there was a knock at her hotel room door. "That was quick!" she mumbled to herself before opening the door without looking through the peephole.

"Richard?" she shouted, "what in the world are you doing here?"

"Hello to you too," he said as he walked past her with his bag in hand. She closed the door behind him, and he set his bag on a nearby chair. "Well, this is nice. This is very nice," he said as he looked around the suite.

"Where the hell did you come from, and how did you know I'd be here? As a matter of fact, how do you even know what room I was in?"

"I'm an FBI agent darling, but I told the clerk I was your husband and I wanted to surprise you for our anniversary." He smiled, took off his jacket, tossed it onto his bag, and sat on the edge of the bed.

"Funny," Evelyn said as she rolled her eyes and went back to the chair and sipped on her wine. "Why the hell are you here? I don't have time for games."

"Well, first off, you stopped answering your phone. And secondly, I told you that we need to talk."

"Yeah, we do need to talk," she said.

"Finally, she agrees with me," Richard said.

"What we need to talk about is why you have someone following me and Camille when you knew that we were here on vacation? This is just like you, Richard; you always have to be in control of everything."

"Look, I'm sorry it was stupid of me, and I wasn't thinking-"

"Do you ever think?" Evelyn interrupted.

"I didn't come here to argue with you; you know I love you, and I was only looking out for your best interest."

"Really? So, having me followed is you looking out

for me or having my best interest? That's what you call love? Please." She scoffed.

"You don't have to believe me, but you know how you are. It's like trouble follows you everywhere you go."

"Yeah, except for when you hire them," She said, pouring herself another glass of wine. "I'm tired right now, you want some?" she said, offering him the bottle.

"Listen to me very clearly," he said as he took the bottle and rested it down on the table beside Evelyn. "I didn't know that this man was going to hurt you and Camille. I didn't know that he was going to kill anybody for that matter. I just wanted you to be safe. And, Camille told me about the roses and the notes that you guys found."

"Thanks for keeping a secret Camille," Evelyn snarked, as she looked up at the ceiling.

"Don't. She's only worried about you, just like I was."

"Yeah, I get it," Evelyn said.

When the food finally came, Richard went to the bathroom and took a shower while Evelyn sat quietly and ate her food. Then she tried ringing Camille again, but there was still no answer to her phone, so she decided to send her a text.

Two minutes later, her phone buzzed, and she thought it was Camille texting her back, but it wasn't. It was Anthony. He told her that he was sad to see her go and wished he could have seen her to say goodbye. She decided not to return the text and put the phone back on the table.

"Something smells good," Richard said as he emerged

from the bathroom with a towel wrapped around his waist and water beaming from the light on his chest. She had forgotten how good he looked and how much she had missed him.

"I left some for you, in case you were hungry."

"No, thank you. I ate already, and I don't want to deprive you of your dinner. I know how you like your seafood."

"Tell me something, Richard. Who is Claude, and where did you meet him?"

"Well, that's a long story, and Claude probably isn't his real name anyway."

"What do you mean?" Evelyn asked.

"I had a background check done on him, and we couldn't find anything, no social security number, no address, nothing, it's like he just appeared out of nowhere. Evelyn, I should have known better. He helped me out with some stuff, and he agreed to do me this favor, and I assumed he was trustworthy. I don't know what he's after, and I certainly don't know why he is after you."

"So, what now?"

"So, now we go back home, and we figure this whole thing out. We catch him and question him and see what else he is after. Plus, I have no idea where he is right now; he stopped answering my calls."

"Camille said he went back to the States.; she didn't say much because the phone got cut off before she could say anything more. I just assumed her phone died or something."

"What? She didn't tell me anything, the last thing I

158

told her was to try and locate your whereabouts," he paused. "I'm sorry, there I go again trying to control you, huh?"

"It's fine. I get it; I'm a loose cannon. I'm always getting into trouble right, and you and Camille are always right there to bail me out. Well, you don't have to babysit me anymore, Richard."

"I didn't say that," Richard responded.

"You didn't have to say it; I've heard it all my life. From my parents, my ex-husband, now you and Camille. I'm a big girl, Rich; you don't have to worry about me. They have tried many times to take me out, but I'm still, here aren't I? and I'm definitely not going anywhere."

"Wait, what do you mean they? Who are they?"

"Look, don't worry about it, I'm tired."

Evelyn's phone buzzed again, and she picked it up without looking at the caller ID assuming it was Camille. "Camille, Hey, what's going on? Oh, I'm sorry, I thought-wait a minute, what? Okay, we'll be on the first thing flying out in the morning, try not to worry ok?"

"What's going on Ev? Who was that?"

Evelyn stared at the phone, she tried to answer Richard, but the words couldn't get to her mouth.

"Evelyn!" Richard rested his hand on her shoulder. "What is it?"

"It's Ca-Camille," she stuttered. "She's missing."

BOOK II

CHAPTER 28

"WHAT I DON'T UNDERSTAND IS, HOW CAN CAMILLE be missing? Are you sure you heard right?" Richard asked Evelyn as they boarded the plane to head back to the United States.

"Her husband said she was supposed to pick up their daughter at her mom's house so that her mom could go to work, but she never showed up. He's been calling and calling her, and she never answered. I'm worried about her Rich. I have been trying to call her all night last night, too, and she never returned my call or my texts. Oh, my God! I just had a horrible thought, what if Claude has her?"

"Don't worry, I'm sure she's alright," Richard said, trying to reassure her. "What exactly did she tell you when you spoke to her last?"

"That's the thing; she didn't say much. She told me she found out that Claude was back in the United States and then she was about to say something else, but the phone got cut off, and I thought that her battery had died. What if she was in danger Rich and it's all because of me? If something happens to her, I could not forgive myself."

"Listen, I'm sure she knows what she's doing. We won't know exactly what happened until we land and hit the ground running. Evelyn, I really want you to come back to work. I don't know why you ever left." Richard said.

They finally boarded the plane and found their seats, and it so happened that their seats were next to each other, Evelyn had a window seat, and Richard sat near the aisle.

"Are you kidding me? Did you plan this?" Evelyn asked Richard.

"No, I promise I had no idea. But I don't think it's a coincidence," he grinned.

"I know exactly where you are going with this, so don't start," Evelyn said.

They settled into their seats; Richard pulled out his laptop, and Evelyn took out a book that she picked up from the airport kiosk. They sat in silence for a few minutes waiting for the rest of the passengers to board the plane.

Richard had asked the passenger that was supposed to sit between them to exchange seats; he wanted to sit next to Evelyn and catch up on the past few weeks.

It was 20 minutes later, and they were in the air, Richard was typing away on his Surface laptop while Evelyn continued reading her book. Although she was looking at the words, her mind was wandering because she was thinking about Camille. *If that man did anything to her. I swear to Go-* she thought to herself,

"You okay, Ev?" Richard asked without looking up from his laptop.

"No, not really," she sighed.

"She'll be fine. Don't worry...she's probably back home by now."

"Are you reading my mind?"

"No, but I know you, and I know how much you care for the people you love."

"If you know me so well, why would you think I would like the idea of being followed? And by a psycho of all people."

"Touché," Richard said, laughing. "I guess I don't know you as much as I would like to. What happened between us Ev? What did I do to make you hate me so much? Is it because I'm your boss? You know we can change that; I can ask to be reassigned to another unit. But I just want to know what happened."

Evelyn closed your eyes and took a deep breath. "I just realized that I needed a break from the relationship, you are a great guy Rich, but I wasn't ready for anything serious, and I know that you wanted more than just a casual fling with me. I guess I couldn't handle it and instead of telling you, I ran away. I'm good at running; I'm not good at being sentimental."

Richard leaned into her and gently held her chin. "You should have told me, we could have talked about it and I would not have come on too strongly, but I do care a lot for you, and I want the best for you."

"I understand," Evelyn said.

"So, what happens now?" Richard asked her.

"What do you mean?"

"Well, when we solve this thing and when we find Camille, and we are going to find her safe and sound, I would like for us to start again. Maybe we can start with just a friendly dinner or coffee?" Richard said, then he put his hands up. "No pressure," he continued, laughing.

"Give me some time to think about it, okay?"

"Okay, fair enough. And what about you coming back to work?"

"With you as my boss? I dunno, Rich. You think you can handle me, seeing as how I'm so difficult to work with?"

"Are you kidding me? You are a great agent and profiler. You were the best."

"I will definitely think about that too. Well, after we finish this case."

She had some things she definitely had to think about after this case.

She took up a magazine and flipped through it and came upon a picture of a woman in a wedding dress on a beach. When she was a little girl, she always wanted to have a real wedding. She dreamt about walking down the aisle with her dad and her husband to be waiting for her at the altar. There would have been two to three hundred people there looking at her and saying how beautiful she was in her wedding dress--though, she wasn't sure where she would have found 200 people. Then, after they said 'I do' they would ride off on a white horse into the sunset.

But that never happened. She didn't have a white dress or a white horse, and her father didn't walk her down the aisle. Her wedding day was dull, she wore a two-piece white suit and stood before a justice of the peace with two witnesses. That was the least romantic day ever, but she was happy. She was happy because she was marrying the man of her dreams, that is until he changed and became the man of her nightmares.

She looked over at Richard who had begun to dose off, and she wondered what kind of husband he would have made if they had ever stayed together. She knew he would never hit her, or any other woman for that matter. He was sweet, kind, considerate, and he truly loved Evelyn. She was foolish for not taking him seriously. She almost wanted to kick herself for making a huge mistake by walking away. But she can't forget the fact that he still hired someone to follow her to the Caribbean and she was still upset with that. How could she let that go?

She nudged him in his arm. "Hey, you asleep?"

"Nope," Richard said with his eyes still closed, "I'm just resting my eyes, Beautiful," He smiled.

"You've never called me that before, where did you get that? Did Ca..." she stopped herself. She didn't want to slip up and talk about Anthony. Anthony was the only person to call her beautiful; it was like a nickname for him. But she was sure Camille wouldn't have told that to Richard. No, why would she? "Never mind." She said.

166

"What? Tell me," he said as he opened his eyes and turned towards her.

"No, it's not important, but I want to know something. Where did you meet Claude, if that is his real name?"

"Well, I was coming out of the gym one night, and my tires were flat, and he helped me. And you know the weirdest thing? I didn't think about it at the time, but it was as if he was waiting for me outside. Don't get me wrong, I am not paranoid, but I know almost everyone at the gym, and everyone knows me. But I have never seen this guy there before."

"Go on." Evelyn nodded.

"Anyway, I offered to buy him a beer, and we went out a couple of times after work. But when you and I broke up, I started getting death threats at the office."

"What? Are you serious?"

"Wait, I never told anyone because I didn't take it seriously, but I guess I should have. I did tell Claude, and I told him about you. I figured that it would be better for him to keep an eye on you because I can handle myself."

"So, what happened to the threats?"

"They just stopped out of the blue, and I didn't think about them until just now. And now I'm starting to think that the threats weren't meant for me."

"You know better, Rich; you're an FBI agent. You should have been more careful. I still can't believe you got that guy to follow me, but now I understand and thanks for telling me."

"Yeah, I told him to follow you Ev, but when I spoke to him the last time, he had a different agenda."

"Wait, what do you mean?"

"He wanted you dead, Evelyn. He knows who you are."

"Richard?"

"Yeah, Ev?"

"That means he knows where I live. He knows where we all live."

CHAPTER 29

CLAUDE SAT IN THE CAFÉ ACROSS THE STREET AND watched the woman enter the apartment building. He first noticed her at the front door, and then she walked a few feet when the elderly man and woman came out before she entered. He didn't want to take any chances and follow her; he didn't want to risk being seen although he wasn't sure if she knew how he actually looked.

He wondered what she was doing, did she get to his apartment already? He was a genius to leave bread crumbs. The cell phone location, leaving it in a location where he knew they would look was sheer brilliance. He would always be steps ahead of them. He knew that someone would come to the building, but he was hoping it was Evelyn, but the sweet dear friend Camille Somble was just as good.

Yes, he knew their names. He knew all of their names. Richard Elias, Camille Somble, and dear sweet Evelyn Rose Dubois. The woman he was after, the only woman he wanted to hurt. He didn't really care about the others, but somehow, he had to use them to get to her. Evelyn. This woman had ruined his life, had taken everything from him, and he was going to do the same thing to her. He was going to take away the most important things in her life first, her friends, then her job, then her life.

Yes.

He also knew where they lived. When they were sleeping at night thinking that all was well with the world, he went through their homes, watched them sleep, and studied them. He remembered when he went into Camille's home, listened to her phone conversation with who he thought was Evelyn on the other end of the line. She was trying to get her to come home. He watched her sleep. He watched her children sleep--the sweet children. He didn't harm children, that was his rule, but he had no problem hurting women. He had no issues hurting Evelyn. He thought about putting a gun to her head and pulling the trigger. That would be too easy. He needed her death to be slow and painful; he wanted to hear her scream. He wanted her to beg for her life before he took it.

He watched and waited and glanced at his watch a few times. He wondered what Camille was doing now. He smiled to himself and sipped the cup of coffee he was holding. He wondered if the agent had found his trophy wall yet.

Everything that he did he made sure was well planned out and timed perfectly. He didn't care that Evelyn finally saw his face, knew what he looked like, that was all in his plan. But he had slipped up a little bit back in the islands. He had lost them for several days. He had drunk too much and made Evelyn tie him up to his bed. It all worked out fine in the end. Evelyn was headed back to the United States, soon.

Minutes later, he watched as Camille sprinted out of the building almost colliding with a boy on a bike. She dug into her pocket and pulled out what looked like car keys and ducked inside her car.

"Shit!" Claude said under his breath. He quickly got up from the table, took a few dollars from his wallet, threw it down, and flew out of the door. He needed to follow her. "What the hell was she up to now? Did she figure it out? Does she know who he was? NO!" he flung his car door open and proceeded to follow her. It took him a while to catch up to her, and when he did, he made sure to stay three cars behind her so that she didn't notice him.

They both drove for miles.

'Where is she going?' Claude said to himself. He didn't anticipate this one at all. He had anticipated that she would find his trophy wall then call Evelyn from wherever she was, and he would capture them, and take them both if he had to. But that wasn't happening. He was now chasing a woman around the country and had no clue where she was going or what she was going to do.

Hours passed, and the only time she had stopped was to fill up her car with gas. He pulled in right behind her and also filled up. He was sure she didn't notice him because she had moved in and out of the store--like light-ening--in what seemed like mere seconds.

"What are you up to Mrs. Somble, and where is Evelyn? Are you going to meet her? Did you call her and tell her about my secret trophy wall?"

* * *

Camille stopped along the street, got out, fed the meter, and then went into the printing shop.

"Hey, Ed. I need to borrow your car for a while; I have an errand to run," Camille said. Ed was her brother-in-law who was married to her sister.

"Leah's mini is out back," Ed said, throwing her the keys and she then threw him hers.

"Thanks a lot, bro," she said and raced out the back door, unlocked her sister's minivan and screeched down the path out of the parking lot towards the main road.

She looked in her rearview mirror; there was no sign of the grey SUV now. She had noticed the vehicle following behind her, making sure not to be noticed, but Camille noticed everything. She wasn't an undercover FBI agent for nothing. She had switched lanes just to make sure that she wasn't simply paranoid. However, when the guy switched lanes too, she knew for sure that she was being followed, and she had an idea as to who was following her. It had to be Claude, she thought to herself.

She had to think quickly; she had no time to waste. That's when she saw the sign to Ed's Printshop. BINGO!

Now she was racing down a street careful not to go too much over the speed limit; the last thing she wanted to do was get stopped by a cop. There was no time now for explanations.

Thirty minutes later and she was outside her friend's house. Her phone buzzed in her pocket. She took it out and looked at it and let it go to voicemail, then she put it on silent, got out of the car and took the stairs two at a time before reaching the front door.

"Hey," She said as a short, dark-haired, skinny woman answered the front door. She looked like she wasn't more than 25 years old, but she was older than that and experienced even.

"Hey yourself," the young woman said.

"Thanks for seeing me, I really appreciate this Lindsey."

"Hey, it's not like I get company every day. Plus, I needed a break," Lindsey said winking at Camille. "What's up?"

"Evelyn's in trouble, and I need you to help me help her," Camille said.

"Come in," Lindsey said then rolled her eyes and shut the door behind them. Lindsey wasn't a huge fan of Evelyn, as a matter of fact, she believed that Evelyn got her fired from the FBI as a computer analyst.

"I know that she isn't your favorite person in the world Linds, but you would be helping to save a person's life, you would be helping the FBI," Camille finished.

"So, she still doesn't know about you, huh?"

"No, I would like to keep it that way. She would

probably hate me if she did. I can't risk that. Right now, she doesn't trust anybody, and I wouldn't want to be next on that list."

Lindsey peered outside, locked the door and turn towards Camille, "Come on. We can work in the basement," she said.

"Paranoid much?" Camille joked as she followed her down a dark hallway then down the stairs to the basement.

"Hey, whatever is going on with the two of you, I don't want to get involved, and I don't want to die, at least not today. You sure no one followed you here?"

"I'm positive," Camille nodded.

Once they were in the basement, Lindsey turned on a light and exposed a computer with four different monitors, and what looked like a server in the corner.

"What in the world... how are you affording all this?"

"Don't ask questions you don't want to know the answer to, just know I'm sending you a huge bill in the mail for this."

"That's fine. Here," Camille said, giving her the photograph that she had taken from the wall at Claude's place.

"Holy Shit! Is that for real?" Lindsey screamed.

"Of course not. Well, I don't think so. I want to know if you can tell me if you recognize anything significant about this picture, where it was taken, blah, blah, blah. You know the drill, so work your magic."

"And I'm betting you want fingerprints too, huh?"

"Well, I wouldn't ask..."

"Boom!" Lindsey said, interrupting her and pulled out a blue light scanner from under her desk that detects fingerprints on objects.

"That would be awesome Linds. You were the best computer analyst we had. Why don't you consider coming back to the FBI?"

"Oh no, uh uh. And work with that mean woman? I would slit my wrist first. Plus, I'm making loads more money here than I would ever make working for you chums."

"Fine. How long is this going to take?"

"Couple hours, maybe a day maybe two, depends on how much I like you," Lindsey grinned.

"Ooooh, let me guess. You charge by the hour, right?"

"Bravo!" Lindsey said as she hit several keys that turned on her computer system.

"You're enjoying this, aren't you?" Camille asked.

"Damn right, I am," she said while she continued punching the keys on the computer. There were codes and names and number that Camille didn't understand; all she could do right now was sit and watch and let the woman work.

"So why is Evelyn in trouble?" Lindsey asked her fingers still typing away at the keyboard.

"We, I mean I, think that someone from her past, when she was in the FBI is trying to hurt her and I'm not sure why or who. He's like a ghost, one minute he's there the next he's not." Camille said.

She told Lindsey about their vacation to St. Thomas

and about the black roses that they found but left out the more personal details.

"I don't even think that Claude is his real name. I would love to get some background information on him as well, but with that name, I'm pretty sure that would be a dead end." Camille said.

"I got you, Cam. Just let me see what I can do. Remember, I'm not doing this for Evelyn, you know how much I hate that woman, but I don't want to see her dead either. I have a heart beating inside this chest, you know?" Lindsey tapped on her chest a few times.

"Well, that is good to know," Camille said.

Four hours later and Camille had dozed off on a sofa across the room. Lindsey shouted, "Voila!" which caused her to jump up. She had almost forgotten where she was for a minute.

"Wait, what's happening?" Camille asked, rubbing her eyes.

"Welcome back, sleeping beauty, I have some information for you."

Camille jumped to her feet and rushed over to the desk and sat down next to Lindsey. "That was quick. Tell me what you got."

"Well, I found out who your ghost or mystery man is." She said, making air quotes. "And his name is certainly not Claude Amos.

"What? I knew it," Camille said, leaning in closer to the screen. "Who is he?"

Lindsey pointed to the screen and leaned back in her chair and smiled as if she had done something great.

On the screen, there were different pictures all of them of Claude and all of them different alias. The last picture made her gasp.

'It all makes sense, now,' She whispered to herself. "Can you make me a copy of everything that you find?"

"Done and Done," Lindsey said while handing her a folder.

Camille's phone buzzed in her pocket again, and she took it out. "Shit, seven missed calls, my husband is going to crucify me I was supposed to be home hours ago. Thank you so much girl, you're the best. I really do appreciate you."

Yeah, Yeah, Yeah, go and catch some bad guys, huh?" Lindsey said. "Remember, your bill will be in the mail."

Camille waved her hand at Lindsey and raced up the stairs and ran through the front door. She couldn't believe her eyes when she got to her sister's car.

"No, No, No. This can't be happening!" she shouted.

CHAPTER 30

AFTER RICHARD AND EVELYN COLLECTED THEIR luggage at the airport, the first stop was to get dinner, then drop off the luggage at Evelyn's house, and then head right over to Camille's house.

Two hours later, both of them were standing on the porch of Camille's house in White Plains. Richard reached for the doorbell and rung it. The door opened, and Camille stood in front of them with her daughter in her hand.

"What the hell, girl? We were so worried about you. They said you were missing," Evelyn said, and she leaned in and hugged her friend.

"I'm okay. I had a flat tire, and my phone died, so I was stuck for a couple of hours trying to get that dealt with. But, I'm not missing. Who said I was missing?"

"It doesn't matter; you're here. You're not missing, and we need to talk."

Closing the door behind them, Richard, Camille, and

Evelyn moved into the living room, and Camille motioned for them to sit while she took her daughter into another room. Five minutes later, she was returned and sat across from the two.

"What's going on guys?" Camille asked.

"What do you mean what's going on, we have a crazed lunatic on the loose, I thought he came after you, we were so worried that we took the first thing smoking so that we could come back and find you and now you're here as if nothing has happened," Evelyn said.

She looked across at Richard, who just sat with his feet crossed and said nothing. He was staring at his phone. How could he be checking messages at a time like this, she thought to herself.

"Ev, I'm fine, I told you."

"Well, we need to find this guy and find out what he's after and fast."

"I agree, Ev. But I don't know what we can do at this point; we don't know anything about him," she lied.

"Well I brought some things back with me so we can get some DNA, we need to do something. We can't just sit back and wait until something bad happens."

Camille nodded but said nothing. She glanced over at Richard, who was still eyes-down in his cell phone. "Hey Rich, can I speak with you for a minute?"

"Sure," he said, looking up from his phone.

When they both got to the kitchen, Camille pulled out an envelope from a drawer and slid it over to Richard.

"I got something. I didn't want to say anything in front of Ev before I told you," Camille said.

"What did you find?" Richard asked.

"Well, I found out where Claude lives, and I went to his apartment. You wouldn't believe me if I told you, Rich. I found his trophy wall. He had photos of Evelyn, of you, and these photos go way back--I'm thinking months, maybe even years.

"Wait, you found out where he lives? How?" Richard said in a whisper.

"Don't worry about it. I have my sources."

"Where does he live?"

She told him the address of the street and apartment number. "I'm not sure if he lives there. And that's not all; I found a picture of Evelyn posed like she was dead in a casket with the words RIP over it. And a black rose in her hand.

"Oh, my God!" Richard said, looking behind him to make sure that Evelyn was not in earshot.

"And, his name is not even Claude, he has maybe five or six aliases dating all the way back into the 90s. This man is dangerous. He could be standing right in front of us now, and we probably wouldn't know it was him. I think we should tell Ev."

Richard rubbed his head and covered his face. "No, not yet, I don't want her going after this guy by herself. You know how she gets lost in these things. Let's just tread lightly for now, Ok?"

"I don't know Rich. You know what happened when we tried to keep things from her."

"Yeah, I know. Let me handle it," Richard said.

They both went back into the living room and saw

Evelyn typing on her phone. She looked up from her phone.

"What is it?" Evelyn said.

"We found a location for Claude," Richard said, sitting next to her on the couch.

"What?" Evelyn said almost leaping out of the chair. "Where?"

"Look, Ev. I want you to let me handle this from here on out. I have guys that can follow him. He knows all of us, and he probably knows that we are on to him by now. He is not stupid," Richard said.

"I'm not going to sit back and just let this man terrorize me and get away with it."

"Ev, let Rich take care of it," Camille said, putting a hand on her friend's shoulder.

Evelyn sighed and smiled. She wasn't smiling because she agreed to what they said. She was smiling because she had what she needed. While they were in the kitchen, Evelyn was listening around the corner. She heard everything. She even got the address and was putting it in her cell phone when they came back into the room. Her anger was just a show.

"Fine, I'll stay out of it." Evelyn finally said.

"Now wait a minute, I don't want you to stay out of it, I can still use your help, I just don't want you running around like a loose cannon and getting into all kinds of trouble," Richard said. "And in the meantime, I am going to get protection for you and Camille around the clock until we catch Claude."

"And you?" Camille said.

"I'll be okay, I know what the man looks like, and I seriously don't think he will come after me unless I got in his way. I think Evelyn is his target." As soon as he said those words, he regretted them. Evelyn was the target? But why? Why had a man he had hired to follow Evelyn to make sure that she didn't get into any trouble, how did he turn on them? He felt like this was all his fault.

"Rich?" Camille said and jostled him out of his thoughts. "You okay?"

"Yes," he said and waved his hand gesturing for her not to worry about him.

"So, what are we supposed to do now?" Evelyn said.

"For now, I need you to go home and get some rest, and we can start fresh first thing in the morning."

"I'm not tired, Richard."

"I know that, but I would still like you to rest so you can be alert and ready for whatever happens tomorrow, I don't want you crashing on me."

"Fine," Evelyn said, throwing up her hands.

"Look, Ev. Go home and get some sleep. I will check up on you later and come get you in the morning, okay? Then we can grab a quick bite to eat, and you can tell me about your trip," Camille winked at Evelyn.

"Okay, so it's settled then. I have to run to the office to clear up some things. But Ev, I can drop you off first, okay?"

"Sure," Evelyn said.

When they pulled up in front of Evelyn's house, there was an undercover agent parked across the street.

Richard had called him on the way, and by the time they had arrived, he was already waiting outside.

Richard stopped by the car to say a few words to the agent. She tried to see who it was, but she couldn't see him because Richard was blocking them.

"Crap!" she whispered. How was she going to sneak around this guy when she doesn't know what he looked like? She was starting to feel tired, and she needed a glass of wine. She hadn't gotten a text from Anthony in hours, and she wasn't sure if she should message him again. But she did miss him and wished he were here with her, whispering in her ears, and kissing her all over. "Get a grip Ev. He has a woman already," she scolded herself.

As soon as Evelyn got into the house, she got undressed and went straightway into the shower, allowing the water to embrace her entire body. It was the break that she needed. She thought about St. Thomas, she missed that island and the hotel. She thought about Claude and wondered what he was doing. She remembered hearing Richard say that he was smart, but he wasn't smarter than her.

Hours later, at midnight, Evelyn was sitting in her car across from Claude's apartment building.

CHAPTER 31

Evelyn had planned to stay awake by drinking cups of coffee she made at home and carried in a thermos. She kept checking the time on her dashboard, and only minutes had passed since she last checked. *This is going to be a long night,* she thought to herself. So far there had been no movement in the apartment, a few lights were on, but there was nothing to indicate life on the inside.

Where was Claude and what was he doing tonight? Was he staking out her house as she sat here? Was he inside making coffee and watching an old movie? Evelyn remembered overhearing Richard and Camille in the kitchen talking about a trophy wall. Why did he have a trophy wall, and why was she on it? All these questions flooded her mind as she mentally searched for answers.

"Who are you, Claude? And what do you want with me?"

She switched on the radio and listened to an old song that she remembered from her childhood. It was Michael

Jackson. She loved his music; she would put on the radio in her room as a child and sing at the top of her lungs using her hairbrush as a microphone.

Her body swayed to the music, and she took out her thermos with the coffee, poured some into a cup, and sipped on it. Right about now she wished that she was drinking wine instead.

She could imagine Camille and Richard screaming at her at the top of their lungs when they found out what she was up to, how she had slipped past her protective detail while he got out of his car to take a piss. She was watching the vehicle for most of the night being careful not to be seen. They would be furious, but she had to see for herself; she had to know why Claude was following her and why he wanted her dead. She had gone over and over this in her mind. Was this a past case, was it someone she knew from a past life?

The only person that she knew who would want her dead was her ex-husband that was the only thing that would explain the roses being left at the hotel. But it was impossible. She went to the funeral; she watched them put the coffin into the ground and cover it with dirt. Was he in the coffin?

Yes.

She had killed him. She had watched him die. She had watched as the blood spewed all over the basement floor. He wasn't breathing. Was he? Did she really kill him? She couldn't be sure now. She had passed out and woke up in the hospital days later. She never asked how she got into the hospital. She never asked if her husband was dead; she just assumed that he was. He was a terrible man, and he deserved to die. But he couldn't come back from the dead. That was just not possible.

Evelyn's mind raced, and her head started to pound. The realization started to kick in. Her husband had sent this man to kill her, or maybe he did it before he died. There was no way he could have known he would have died that night. She had to know; she had to be certain. She would wait until Claude left the apartment then she would go in and look around. She had to know the truth even if it killed her.

Evelyn had been in a deep sleep when she heard a knock on her car glass that made her jump. "What the-" she gathered her thoughts quickly. It took her a moment to realize where she was and what she was doing there. The banging on the window continued. She turned a saw a dark figure standing outside her window with a hoodie covering their head.

"Shit!" Was that Claude? Had she been made? A string of curses escaped her lips again. It was now or never; she had to know. She slowly rolled down the glass when she noticed him.

"What the hell are you doing here, Ev? Gotdammit...I knew you would do something like this!" Richard shouted into the car but not so loud as to wake the neighborhood. "I gave you one simple instruction, and you couldn't follow it."

"Were you following me? I can't believe you some-times," Evelyn said, feeling annoyed.

"Me? Follow you? There I was in my bed asleep

when I get a call from my guy who was supposed to be guarding your house. And you know what he tells me? Evelyn is missing. So, I tell him to sit tight and see if she comes back. But no, she never comes back. I decide to get out of my warm bed and go over to your house to see for myself."

"You don't have to talk to me like that, Richard. I'm not a child."

"Really? Because you have been nothing but a pain in my ass since this whole thing started. Are you really trying to get yourself killed?" he sighed.

"I needed to see for myself, and I'm not going to sit back and be babysat by you or anybody. I'm a part of this investigation too, Rich."

Richard glared at Evelyn through the glass. He wanted to say more to her, but he was tired and was starting to get a headache from a lack of some much-needed sleep. He would let her have the rest in the morning.

"Go home Ev," he said, irritated.

"Listen," she said, but Richard interrupted her.

"I'm not going to tell you again. Go, home!" Richard said, before storming off, getting back into his car, and speeding away.

Evelyn was furious. Why can't people see that she was a grown woman, and she could handle herself? She was not about to do what Richard told her. She wasn't a child, and she certainly wasn't his woman anymore. Who did he think he was talking to her like that?

She was tired of waiting; she had to move now.

Evelyn dug into her glove compartment, removed her gun, and secured it in the back of her jeans. She looked around and then pulled up her hoodie over her head. She opened the car door and made a dash across the street towards Claude's apartment building.

She tried the front door. It was locked.

Glancing at her watch, she noted that it was now after 2 a.m. It would be crazy to push the buzzer and wake anyone up at this hour.

"Think Evelyn, think." She scolded herself under her breath. The only thing she could do now was to wait until someone came out of the apartment, but she hated waiting. Why couldn't she just get this over with?

Her prayer must have been answered because a few minutes later, she heard a buzz and a click, the door swung open, and a young couple exited the building laughing and talking. They didn't notice Evelyn, and she was able to slip past them and enter the building. She could smell alcohol, and they reeked of marijuana.

She found the staircase and slowly climbed them until she reached the third level and softly pulled the exit door open. She was standing in a dimly lit hallway, and she looked up and down to make sure that no one was around. She paused. Nothing.

When she reached Claude's door, she pulled the gun from her waistband and waited, listening for any noise inside. Slowly, she turned the doorknob, and to her surprise, it was unlocked. Raising her gun, she slowly stepped inside the apartment. It was empty.

No Claude.

A mattress was in the center of the room, papers scattered on the floor, along with books and trash. It was a mess. There was a desk with computer screens. She went over to the computer and tapped the keyboard; the screens lit up, but it was password protected.

She rifled through the drawers to find something about him, identification, passport anything that would tell her who he was. Nothing. She was so consumed by the task that she didn't even notice his footsteps behind her.

CHAPTER 32

THE PAIN TO THE BACK OF EVELYN'S HEAD NAGGED AT her until she was forced to open her eyes and realize that she was in complete darkness. She thought she had gone blind for a second, and panic swept all over her body. It was like Deja vu all over again, only this time she wasn't bound, but her limbs felt heavy. It was almost impossible for her to move. What was happening? What had he done to her? Her head began to throb, and she could feel her heart pounding in her ears. Claude had probably hit her with something that made her lose consciousness. Why hadn't she seen or heard him coming up behind her?

All she remembered was searching his apartment. It was a trap; it had to be. It was like he knew that she was going to be there somehow. The realization hadn't hit then that if she was watching his apartment, then he was definitely watching her--following her as he had done in the islands. How did she get to be so stupid? She was so caught up in the case that she let him get inside her head.

She lost her focus.

Closing her eyes for a moment and taking a few slow, steady breaths, she heard the familiar voice inside her head, *Think Evelyn, you are not going to die here.* The voice said it again. *You are not going to die here.* It was hers. It was her voice.

She opened her eyes again and blinked a couple of times to adjust to the darkness. "Maybe if I could get to a door, just maybe I could find a way out." But she didn't know where she was or how she had gotten there. Was she even in the same building? Did they somehow leave? Are they even in the same city? She didn't know. She wasn't even sure if it was the same day.

She felt a single tear run down her cheek, and she tried to lift her hand to wipe it away, but her arm was numb, and it was as if she was lifting a ton of bricks. She groaned. What had he done to her? The pain at the back of her head was beginning to become unbearable. What the hell did he hit her with? The pain seemed to be traveling, down her neck to her back. She tried to move her legs, but they too were feeling numb. She tried again and again until she was finally able to lift her right hand slowly and move it across her half-naked body. She wasn't wearing any clothes. He skin was a bit sticky to the touch.

"No, no, no." she cried; this is not happening again.

Her heart began to race again as she was starting to put the pieces together. A void filled in her memory, and she suddenly remembered how she got there. She remembered the moving car, she remembered opening and closing her eyes as they passed street lights and houses. She remembered being in the back seat of a car, with something covering her body and her face, but she only saw silhouettes and light shone through the fabric. She heard music, a man on the radio.

She didn't know where he had taken her, and no one would know where she was this time. She should have listened to Rich and Camille. If she wasn't dead already, Richard would kill her himself. She heard his voice, "Go home, Evelyn, you are going to get yourself killed." He was right; he was always right.

She looked around the darkness again for a way out or some kind of light. She wasn't going to die in there. She had to keep reminding herself that she was a fighter; she was stronger than Claude. She squeezed her eyes again and opened them, and then she saw it--a thin bar of light shone through the corner on the opposite end of the room. It was a door, and now there was some glimmer of hope on the inside of her. The door was probably locked, and she couldn't imagine what horror was lying in wait behind it, but all she needed to do right now was to get to the door.

She suddenly developed a strength she didn't know existed, and with both hands, she grabbed hold of the ground and pulled herself across the floor to the other side of the room. The feeling in her arms slowly came back, and the pain became excruciating. She stopped a few times to take a breath and to shake out her arms.

"Come on, Ev," she coached herself. "Please, don't

stop. You're almost there." But it felt like an eternity. Her legs and her body were scraping against the cold hard, pavement, and she could feel the ground cutting away at her flesh. It was hurting her, and another tear escaped her eyes.

If she had listened to Richard, she would not be in this situation right now, she thought. "You are so stubborn sometimes," she heard another voice echo in her head. This time that voice was not her own. "You couldn't just leave it alone. You couldn't just stay away; you always have to be the hero," the voice said. She recognized the voice. It was her husband, her dead husband. He was trying to get inside her head as always, even from beyond the grave. He was always trying to manipulate her.

"Don't listen to him, Ev. He cannot hurt you now; he's gone, you won't ever see him again. You are brave and strong, and you are not going to die here, keep moving, please, you're almost there. Just keep moving!"

She inhaled the musty air and kept her eyes on the light in the corner of the room. She was almost there. She felt the cold hard ground again, and this time, something sharp pierced her side, and she screeched in pain, but she didn't stop. She kept going until the light got closer and closer and bigger and bigger. She didn't stop to take any more breaths, and she ignored the sharp pain in her side. She needed to get out--to be free. It took an eternity, but she finally reached the light, and she propped herself up against the nearby wall to catch her breath.

She closed her eyes for a second to rest. She wondered to herself what kind of God would let her go through this again, this torture and pain. Was this her punishment for not listening to her friends' many stern warnings for her to stay away from this case, from Claude? Was this punishment for her past sins? Were the black roses a symbol of her last days here on earth? What had she done in her previous life to deserve this? All she wanted was to be happy; she had dreams and goals like everyone else. She too wanted the great job, the husband and kids and the house with the white picket fence. Why didn't she deserve that? She had bought this down on herself. With all the training that she had gotten over the years, she should have known better. She should have waited and let the real authorities handle it. She was way in over her head now. She didn't know this man or what he was capable of. She was unprepared for this, and suddenly she was disappointed in her behavior.

But it all would be over soon, and she was getting out, she was going to be free, and she would listen and follow instructions. She groaned as she yearned for something to numb the pain in her head. It seemed to be getting more and more painful.

Her eyes were still closed, and she saw her mother in the distance coming towards her; but the more she came, the further away she seemed. "No, mom. Come back, don't go." She whispered as another tear fell down her cheek.

Her mother was telling her something, but she couldn't understand, she was trying to scream at the top of her lungs, but Evelyn didn't know what she was saying.

"Mom, please come back," She whispered again. Then her mother was gone; she had disappeared into thin air. She sobbed. She couldn't move. Her head hurt, and the pain seemed like it was radiating throughout her whole body. She wished someone would find her and come to her rescue. Somebody, anybody. Where were they? Where was everybody? Were they even looking for her? Do they know that she was missing?

Missing. She willed herself to open her eyes and try for the door. *Come on,* Ev. She heard the voice in her head again. *You have to get up. You have to try and get out of here.*"

"I tried. I can't. I'm not strong enough. I'm too tired, and the pain is too much," she whispered. Then she heard her mother's voice again.

"Evelyn Rose Dubois, you get up from there right now. Don't let me have to tell you again!"

Richard's voice chimed in, "Go home, Ev, you are going to get yourself killed."

Then she heard Camille's voice, "Ev, honey, everything is going to be okay, I'm coming, I'm coming to get you."

Then she heard his voice, the voice that she hadn't heard in years. "My sweet Rose, I love you so much. You are strong, and you are beautiful, just like a rose. Don't give up, baby girl; you can do this," her father said. He always said that to her, she missed him so much now. If Evelyn could only talk to him now, she would say how much she was sorry; sorry for not keeping in touch, sorry for turning her back on him and she would tell him how much she loved him.

When she finally blinked opened her eyes, the horror had set in, and Evelyn realized she had not moved from the spot where Claude had put her, and the light at the bottom of the door in the other corner of the room had moved miles away.

CHAPTER 33

CLAUDE STOOD OVER EVELYN'S BLOODSTAINED BODY and watched her with her eyes closed and her head bent. She looked like she was still unconscious or sleeping. She groaned a few times, and he wondered what was going through her mind. Was she dreaming? He bent down to her and lifted her chin toward him so he could see her face, but she didn't open her eyes. Her lips moved, but no sounds came out. She was dreaming. Maybe he put too much of the drug in the syringe, or he hit her over the head too hard. He didn't care; she had it coming. She had much more coming.

Claude walked over to the middle of the room and grabbed a small bucket and walked back toward Evelyn. He poured ice-cold water over her head. She bolted awake, fighting to catch her breath. She tried to move, but her hands were tied behind her, and her feet were bound together.

He smiled and watched her as she struggled to

breathe, inhaling and exhaling at rapid speeds, making sure not to take in too much water. He bent down and met her gaze.

"What do you want? Please let me go. I'm not the one you want," She panted.

"You are exactly the person I want," he grinned.

"Please let me go. I promise I won't come after you anymore. I won't tell anyone about you. Please," she begged.

Claude laughed. "You really think I'm going to let you go? The only way you're getting out of here is in a coffin. And one that I especially made for you. I will bury you so far out of nowhere that they will never find your body. Then, I will go after your friend Camille and your boyfriend Richie, and you all can have a good ole reunion wherever you end up," he said as he stood up. "I am going to take my time with you, Evelyn Rose Dubois. You are going to feel every single pain that you have coming to you."

"No, Please, just let me go," Evelyn pleaded with him some more, but Claude ignored her pleas.

"Please, no, stop, please, let me go," he taunted her. "Evelyn honey you need to stop begging. You asked for this, you asked for all of this." Claude said.

Claude pulled a knife from his back pocket and held it against Evelyn's cheeks, and she squeezed her eyes shut. Then she felt Claude cut the rope from around her leg, which caused her to open her eyes again. He had loosened her restraints. Was he letting her go? No.

"Get up!" Claude shouted and pulled Evelyn limp

body up to her feet. She was weak and could barely walk. She limped on one foot while the other foot drug behind. But her hands were still bound behind her back. He carried her out of the darkened room and into another room that looked like a kitchen. There was a stove, a small island, a fridge, and a wooden chair in the center of the room. The windows had been boarded up so that she couldn't see outside. Where was she?

Where had he taken her?

Claude threw her down into the wooden chair and walked behind her. She was uneasy and scared because she didn't know what he was going to do next. She couldn't see him. He reappeared with a square, wooden object. He turned it to face her, and she realized it was a mirror.

Horror came over her when she didn't recognize the person that was looking back at her, her face. Claude had slit a long cut on the left side of her face from her head close to her eye right down to her chin.

"Oh, my God! What did you do to my face?" she screamed, her voice now hoarse. "What have you done to me?" Was he going to disfigure her so she would be unrecognizable? She was in a nightmare. This was her nightmare. The pain she was feeling wasn't just her head; it was also her face. The mirror was big enough that she could see most of her upper body. She saw dried blood on her skin. She was in her underwear and noticed a cut on her stomach. Had he stabbed her? Or, was she still dreaming? What was happening?

Claude didn't just want her dead; he was going to

torture her. He was going to deliver enough pain that she would beg him to kill her. Claude was as evil as they come. But what did she do to deserve such agony?

Evelyn stared at her reflection in the mirror, and she blinked several times as the tears began to run down her face. Was she really going to die here? Was this really her time? She had to come to terms with this. She had killed once before, and maybe this was her punishment. She had taken a life, and now her life would be taken.

Claude stood in front of her and smiled.

"I have something for you," he said as he removed his hand from around his back. He was holding a single black rose tied with a purple ribbon. "My sweet Rose, My sweet black rose," he said grinning.

That voice.

He no longer spoke in the low grumbling voice. His voice was familiar to her now, and Evelyn looked up at him in horror. Her heart raced. The room began to spin. "What?' she whispered, but the words barely escaped her lips. "Ronald? No, it can't be."

This man was familiar to her. The face was Claude's, but the voice was definitely her dead husband's. She gazed into his eyes. They had changed too from when they first met back in St. Thomas. Was he wearing contacts before? There was no mistaking those light grey eyes; they were one of the reasons she had fallen for him.

"No! I watch you die. I killed you!" she said.

"Really, Ev? Did you really kill me?"

"I watched them bury you. I was at the funeral, and I watched them put you into the ground and cover you with dirt. I made sure that you were dead, that you wouldn't come back."

"Well, my dear, when you have a lot of money like I do, you pay people to fake your death and have fake funerals; and I did know a lot of people. They owed me big time. Did you really think I was going to let you get away with my murder? Come on now, baby! What kind of a man would I be?"

Evelyn shook her head. "No, I saw you, and I saw the blood."

She did see him die. She was there when they called her to identify his body. She was there when they put the casket into the ground and covered it up with dirt.

"Please, don't do this. People will be looking for me, and they will find me. They will find you. Just let me go," Evelyn pleaded.

"Nobody is looking for you. They won't find you, Evelyn. Do you think they care about you? They don't know the kind of person that you are; they don't know you like I do," Claude shouted at her.

"I'm not the same person you knew," she said.

"You are the same person; you lie, you manipulate people to get what you want, to get your way and when you don't, you hurt them, just like you hurt me."

"That's not me anymore. I'm not the same person."

"You are the same Evelyn I have always known. I have been watching you for months--waiting, and watching. You may not know this babe, but I've got a lot of patience. I watched you and your boyfriend, Richard; how you used him for sex and dumped him when you couldn't get your way. That's how you are Evelyn, that's how you have always been, you never change. I knew about your infidelities with other guys; I knew about the pregnancy. Was the baby even mine Ev?"

"Please, just stop. I'm begging you," She cried.

"Was the baby mine?"

"Yes." She whispered.

"I watched your belly grow and grow, and I waited. Then one day you were back to your old slim self again, and there was no baby. What did you do with the baby Evelyn? Where's my baby? Did you kill my baby Evelyn? Did you kill our baby?"

"No, I didn't," she cried, "I gave him away."

"Him? I have a son?" he stepped back and glared at her. Then he looked off into the distance as if looking at his son. "I have a son." He repeated.

"No, he's not yours; he's better off not being with either you or me. You will never find him."

Claude lifted his hand and hit Evelyn in the face. She screamed out in pain and then cried, "Do what you want to me, but I will never tell you where he is, and you will never see him. You may as well kill me now. I'm don't care anymore. I'm done."

"No, you aren't done until I say you're done. We are just getting started. And the good thing is no one can hear you scream for miles. After this, I will disappear. I can change my identity, I did it before, and I can do it again. It would be like I was never here. Now it's time to pick up where we left off."

CHAPTER 34

Camille tailed Claude's white Chevy from his downtown apartment building in Brooklyn making sure to stay several cars behind so she could not be seen. She had been watching his building that morning and waited all day until he emerged later in the evening and walked out of the building carrying something wrapped in a blanket. She couldn't make out what it was exactly.

She knew that he had figured out what she had done a couple of days before when she got her sister's SUV, and then he tailed her to her friend's house all the way to West Haven, Connecticut. She wondered how he did it. How was it that it seemed like he was always one step ahead? How did he know? She got a different car this time an unmarked black sedan from the FBI parking lot. He would not know what was coming this time.

The night at Lindsey's, they had uncovered Claude's true identity, although he had several aliases. But this time he even went as far as to hire a doctor to change his features. But those eyes. Those eyes didn't lie; there was something about those eyes in those pictures. Of course, he wore disguises in some, a mustache, thicker eyebrows, a fake beard, and glasses. She had taken the very first picture and ran it through the FBI database and the computer exploded with information. His real name was Ronald Gregory Dubois, Evelyn's husband.

Why would a man go through so much trouble not to be found? She had figured out the answer. So that when he killed her, he could disappear without a trace. But he wouldn't get away this time; she knew who he was and how he looked.

But where was Evelyn?

She tried calling Evelyn's cell phone several times earlier that morning and the morning before that to check on her because they had made plans to have breakfast and head to the FBI building, but her phone kept going straight to voicemail. She didn't bother calling Richard this time. She wanted to follow Claude herself. She wanted to know what he was up to before she called Richard in for help. This man was dangerous, and she had no idea what he was going to do once he got his hand on Evelyn, his ex-wife.

Claude seemed like he had been driving for hours. He didn't stop, and he didn't pull over for gas or to get food. He kept the speed limit at a steady pace, he didn't speed up, and he didn't slow down, but he constantly switched lanes now and again. Camille was smart. She tried as much as she could to stay in the same lane and not switch too often. As a matter of fact, she didn't have to switch lanes at all.

Camille had placed a small GPS signal underneath Claude's car just in case she lost him. And she wasn't going to lose him this time. But where was he going?

Maine.

Finally, Claude pulled onto a long-deserted winding dirt road that led to what looked like a farmhouse about a half-mile from the main road. Camille didn't follow him in fear of being seen, so she stayed at the end of the driveway and took out her binoculars.

He made several trips back and forth from his car to the house. Then she noticed him take whatever he had wrapped up inside of the sheet and tossed it over his shoulder and carried it inside. Forty-five minutes later, he came back out of the house and took a huge box from his car and went back inside. Camille looked at her watch and waited. She wasn't sure what she wanted to do next. Should she wait and see what he does next? She took out her cell phone and tried Evelyn again, and when she didn't answer, she left her another message.

"Ev, where are you? I have been trying to reach you all day today, and yesterday, please give me a call. I need to know that you are alright."

She figured Evelyn must have swallowed a bottle of one of her favorite wines and slept it off. But she should have been answering her phone by now. She dialed again, this time it was Richard who answered.

"Hey Rich, have you heard from Evelyn today?" she asked him.

"Not since yesterday, I guess she took my advice and went home, where are you now?"

"I'm a long way outside of the city doing some surveillance."

"Okay, I have a meeting now, so come into my office when you get back and bring Evelyn when you get a hold of her we have some things to take care of."

"Yes, sir," She said as she hung up the phone.

She looked back into the binoculars. Nothing. Claude was nowhere to be seen, but she would wait until it got dark enough then she was going to make her move. He was planning something, she thought to herself. But what was it?

It had been hours since she'd seen any movement from Claude, and darkness was beginning to move in. She would move when it was dark enough. She pulled out her gun from the glove compartment and put it on the passenger seat just in case. Then she waited. She called her husband and her kids and then placed a call to Evelyn's phone again, still no answer.

"Where the hell are you, girl?" she whispered to herself.

Just then, the thought hit her like a brick in the back of her head. Claude must have been carrying a body in the sheet. He was carrying Evelyn.

She remembered the stories that Evelyn told her about Claude when they were in the Islands. He had beaten her several times and even broken a couple of her ribs. She knew that Evelyn wasn't going to leave this case alone. She probably followed him, or he took her from her home while she was asleep. But how? When? How did he get ahold of her?

That means it was Evelyn that he was carrying from the apartment building to his car. 'Oh my God!' she whispered, then peered through the binoculars again. She couldn't imagine what he must have done to her--what he is doing to her now. She had to get her friend out of that house, but it would be suicide if she went in there alone, without backup.

"You don't have time to waste Cam, think, think," she said, pounding her palm against her forehead.

Claude was dangerous, but she didn't know to what extent, but he wasn't that smart. She decided that she couldn't wait any longer if she wanted to save her friend; if she wanted to get him, she had to move now.

She called Richard again; however, this time the call went directly to voicemail. "Rich, it's me. He's got Evelyn." She shouted the address into the phone then hung up and took up the binoculars again. "Where are you, you son of a bitch?" she said.

Camille was not only an undercover agent, but she was an expert sharpshooter. She had spent a few years in the army before she started working in the FBI. She would be able to take him down with one shot from miles away. She just wished the bastard would step outside one last time. But he didn't, and she was growing increasingly impatient.

"Come on Claude, step outside let me see you. Just

one step so I can take your head off." She said as she looked through the binoculars.

She thought for a second. She didn't recall the sheet moving when he was carrying it into the house. Is she dead? Did he kill her already?

"I'm coming Ev, just hold on for me, I'm coming. Everything is going to be alright." She had to believe that. She had to believe that Evelyn was still alive because she would never forgive herself if this man had killed her.

She took her weapon from the passenger seat and softly exited the SUV. She looked around first to make sure that no one was around, then she slowly made her way to the driveway.

She stayed close to the brush and trees that lined the driveway to the house. She stayed low and walked slowly up the path. It seemed like it was taking forever for her to get to the house. There was a rustling in the bushes a few feet ahead that stopped her dead in her tracks. With her gun lifted, she knelt and waited. Was it Claude? Had she been seen?

No.

It took a minute or so for her to realize that it must have been an animal in the bushes. She took a deep breath then let it out again. "Come on, girl, don't get paranoid on me," she said.

She got up and slowly walked towards Claude's parked car. When she finally got to the vehicle, she stooped behind it and listened for any noise or movement from inside of the house — still nothing. Camille crept up to the front of the house and waited and listed again for any sign of movement inside. That's when she heard it... a faint shout or a scream. She wasn't sure, but it sounded like a woman's voice.

Evelyn was still alive.

CHAPTER 35

"You know, Evelyn, we had a lot of fun when we were together; we had a lot of memories too. When I first saw you, I thought to myself, that girl right there, I'm going to make her my wife no matter what. The room just seemed to light up whenever you walked in. You remember that hun, the day that we met?" Claude said as he paced the room.

Evelyn stared into the mirror at her reflection. She saw the tears beginning to flood her eyes again, and she closed them. She did remember when they first met. She had walked into the restaurant with her cousin, and spotted him right away at a table with three other guys; they wore suits and jeans and were talking and laughing. She learned later that they were his co-workers. She thought it was love at first sight when he had come over to their table, all smiles, and introduced himself ; well, until the fights and the beatings began.

"I'm talking to you; do you remember that?"

"Yes," she whispered.

"I can't hear you," he said and grabbed a fist full of hair in his hand and yanked her head back so hard that Evelyn thought she heard something in her neck snap.

"Yes! I remember!" she screamed.

"Good," he said and paced the room again. Then he stopped and looked up at the ceiling. "I thought we would be the perfect couple. We did so much; we've been through so much together. Why did you have to betray me, Evelyn?" he said.

Evelyn felt a sharp pain to the back of her head, and it took her several seconds to realize that he had hit her again. The pain in her body was unbearable now. Where was Camille when she needed her? Where was Richard? Is anybody looking for her? She closed her eyes again and said a silent prayer. She wished that when she opened her eyes again, this would all be a nightmare. She should have listened to Richard. "Go home, Evelyn, you want to get yourself killed?" he had said. Now she wished she had listened to him. No one knew where she was. She didn't even know where she was.

"No, no, no. Don't you dare give up on me, open your eyes. It's not over until I say it's over." Claude hit her in the face this time, and she saw her blood splatter all over the floor.

She didn't know how much more pain she could take. She wasn't built for this kind of torture. Why didn't he just end it all right now? What was he waiting on? Then she heard a voice, a familiar voice, "Ev, don't give up; I'm coming, I'll be right there just hold on." The voice whispered.

"Cam? Is that you Cam?" Evelyn whispered.

She could barely open her eyes, and when she did, the room spun. And Claude was nowhere around. Where did he go? What's he doing now?" she wondered.

Evelyn blinked several times before the room began to come back into focus, but her head was throbbing. She quickly scanned the room. She had to try and get out of here before he got back. But that task was impossible. She was strapped to a chair, she had lost the feeling in both legs, and her head felt like it had been cracked open. She wouldn't have gotten very far even if she had tried to escape. She looked in the mirror again and gasped when she saw Claude staring at her through the mirror. He had this eerie look in his face; he didn't say anything he just stared. But his face was different. What did he do to his face?

"If you're thinking about escaping, don't even bother," he was smiling.

Her eyes widened, and she thought he was reading her mind or had she been talking out loud all this time? She couldn't tell. Whatever drugs he had given her had taken away all her inhibitions. She was afraid of what he was about to do next.

"Now I'm going to have so much fun killing you for everything you put me through," Claude said, holding a knife blade at her neck. And as he pressed harder, she felt the knife slowly begin piercing her flesh.

"No, please," Evelyn whispered.

Claude hit her again on her cheek, and she winced in pain, and she was grateful that the pain wasn't as bad a before.

"No, please... what?" he mocked her.

"I'm so sorry, just let me go," Evelyn pleaded with him again.

"You know Evelyn, this is the first time I have ever killed anyone, I mean I have tortured you before but not like this time. I have given you so much, I really loved you, and you know what you did... you took my love for granted. You went out there with your friends, and you fooled around on me while I worked so hard for us. How do you think that makes me feel?" he hit her again when she didn't answer him. "Answer me!"

"You didn't love me. Was it loved when you broke my rib, and I ended up in the hospital? Was it love when I had three miscarriages because of you? You call that love? I never cheated on you."

"Yes, you did. I followed you, and I saw you with those guys. You think you can sit there and lie to me?"

"I never cheated on you; they were teaching me how to fight; how to defend myself against you. I wanted to hurt as much as you hurt me. I loved you, and you hurt me over and over again."

"So, you wanted to hurt me, huh?"

Claude moved slowly around to face Evelyn and looked her in her face. Then he struck her in her stomach as hard as he could. She heaved and threw up a little blood.

Everything was starting to get cloudy, and the room

started to spin again. Then she realized, he hadn't stuck her in the neck with a knife, he was giving her another injection. The pain wasn't as bad anymore. But now she felt like she was floating in the air, and everything around her seemed calm.

"No," she whispered.

"Let her go now!" the voice startled Claude, and he looked up and saw Camille standing behind him with her gun raised and aimed at his head.

"Well, look who we have here. Have you come to join the party, Camille?" Claude said, throwing his head back and laughing.

"Claude, let her go now, and I won't shoot you in the head! I won't tell you again."

Claude thought for a minute and weighed his options then said: "You kill me, and I kill her. It's that simple, Agent Camille Somble."

Camille furrowed her brow and looked at Claude as he stood in front of Evelyn, who seemed to be unconscious now. He was holding a knife in his left hand and in his right hand, he grabbed a lock of her hair.

"You seemed shocked, Agent," he continued. "You think I didn't know that you were an uncover agent for the FBI? Does Evelyn even know that her best friend in the whole world is an undercover agent?"

Camille said nothing. Her handgun still pointed at Claude.

"How do you think she is going to react when she finds out that you have been keeping a huge secret from her? Wait, hold on, I guess it will have to be our little secret because once she's dead, she will never find out. But you will have to kill me before I ever let her live again."

Camille stepped forward towards them.

"Ah ah ah! You stay right there, or I will slit her throat. You drop the gun now or watch your best friend die," he said, holding the knife firmly against Evelyn's throat.

Camille looked at Evelyn and hoped that she wasn't dead. She wasn't moving, and she had to think fast. "Alright, fine," she said, throwing both of her hands in the air, while still holding onto the gun.

"Drop it. Now!" Claude yelled.

Camille did as he said and dropped the gun a few feet away from her feet. "What did you do to her? Is she dead?"

"Oh not yet, just a very strong sleeping drug, she'll be out just long enough for you to watch me kill and bury her, then I'll take care of you and your friend Richard and your families, then I will disappear." He smiled again.

He stepped away from Evelyn and took two steps towards Camille.

"Well, that's not going to happen."

"And why the hell not?"

"Because you missed something," Camille reached quickly behind her and pulled out her backup gun, pointed it at Claude and without hesitation, pulled the trigger.

CHAPTER 36

CAMILLE STOOD AT THE FOOT OF THE BED IN THE hospital room and watched her friend lying there with IV lines running all over her, after having endured a seven-hour surgery. Evelyn looked so tiny in the bed with her face badly swollen, a couple of fractured ribs, and a concussion. She was lucky to have survived the brutal attack by Claude, and Camille was thankful that she had gotten there just in time.

The doctors told Camille that Evelyn was breathing on her own for now, but it would take a while for her to come out of the coma. Claude had done a real number on her. 'My poor friend,' she thought to herself. She couldn't imagine what had been going through Evelyn's mind while she was being tortured almost to death. "Please, wake up Ev, I'm here. Everything is going to be alright," Camille whispered.

Evelyn's mother sat in a chair next to her bed. She

prayed, and she cried, and she prayed again for her daughter to wake up. She spoke out loud to her, and sometimes Camille just noticed her mouth moving with no audible sound. She wondered what she was saying.

"I always thought that he wasn't good for my Evelyn," Her mother had said to Camille. "She called me one day and said, 'Mom, I got married.' She was so excited, she always wanted to be married, ever since she was a little girl. She would pretend that she was a little bride with her dolls. But I knew in my heart that he wasn't good enough for my sweet Evelyn. But what could I do? What could I have said? I wanted my daughter to be happy. He wasn't good enough, but I didn't want her to hate me. The thing that hurts a mother the most is knowing that your child is in trouble, and you can't do anything to help."

"There is nothing you could have done. Evelyn knows that you love her," Camille said and held Evelyn's mother close. "She has always been a strong woman, and she will get through this. We all will, just you watch and see."

"Thank you for saving my baby, Camille; she wouldn't have been here on this earth without you."

"I love your daughter like she was my own sister."

"I know dear." Camille let go of the embrace, and Evelyn's mom took her napkin and wiped her eyes. "You know, parents should never have to bury their children."

"Don't talk like that now. She will be okay."

Camille wasn't sure if she believed her own words. Looking at her friend in the bed all bandaged up, her breathing shallow. She wished she could have done more. But all she could do now was pray and hope that Evelyn would wake up soon. They both had a lot to talk about. About Claude. About herself.

Camille excused herself to make a call and stepped out into the hallway when she saw Richard exit the elevator. He stopped by the desk to talk to the nurse first before going in to see Evelyn.

Richard was furious when he found out what happened. If Claude hadn't died, he was going to make sure of it. Richard had visited Evelyn when they brought her into the hospital. Camille had never seen him that vulnerable before; she even thought she caught a glimpse of a single tear escape his eye when he saw her lying on the bed.

Camille had flashbacks to the photos that she had taken from the wall in Claude's apartment. It was like she was looking at the exact image of Evelyn except for the wires running through her. She couldn't sleep at nights because she had dreams of Evelyn and Claude in that house-- Claude stabbing Evelyn in front of her, and then coming towards her. She would always fire her gun, but somehow, she would miss, or the bullets would just go through him and disappear. She never had trouble sleeping before, she was good at what she did, but this case was very close to her. Evelyn was family. Why was she having these nightmares? It was over, wasn't it? Claude was dead finally. She made sure of it when she went to the morgue and watched them autopsy the body.

Richard had even ordered to have his body cremated. But it wasn't over, was it?

Was Evelyn still in danger?

"How is she?" Richard asked as he came over to where Camille was standing guarding the room door.

"She's still the same Rich. She hasn't woken up yet. Her mom is still there; she hasn't left her side since she came in here."

"Well, that's good, she needs the support right now," Richard said.

"Are you going to be alright, Rich? I know how much you care for her."

"I'll be fine. I'm just glad that you were there in time to save her life."

"I really wished I could have gotten in there sooner. I should have followed my guts, and I shouldn't have waited."

"Look at me. Don't you go beating yourself up, you did the right thing. Evelyn is going to be alright. She is going to pull through. She's a bit stubborn yes, but that's her. Sometimes you have to take the good with the bad."

"Did you get in contact with her dad?" Camille asked.

"No, I called several times, but he didn't answer. I'm not even sure if he's still in the country. Do you know when she last spoke to him?"

Camille shrugged. "She hardly talks about him at all."

Richard sighed, leaving Camille's side, and went into the room, where he spoke softly to Evelyn's mother who got up and gave him a hug. She was such a nice woman, full of warmth, loving, and cared about everyone around her. Evelyn had some of her mother's qualities in her. Camille suspected that she had a few of her father's qualities in her too. Evelyn just didn't see it; she hated her father so much. When Evelyn opens her eyes, and she will open her eyes, Her mom would be the first person that she sees. She loved her mom so very much.

Camille couldn't hear what Richard was telling Evelyn's mother, but she was nodding and wiping her eyes with her napkin. He kissed her on the cheek and then exited the room and stood next to Camille.

"Everything alright?"

"Yes, I had spoken to the Doctor earlier. He said that Evelyn was going to be alright. She's strong, and her vital signs are improving. He ribs are going to take a while to heal."

"Well, that's good news," Camille said but

Richard frowned.

"What's the matter, Rich? Something bothering you? This is great news; you should be happy that our girl is going to be fine."

"Yeah, I know, but that's not all he said," Richard replied.

Camille was worried now, and she watched Richard look off into the distance. "Is it bad? What's wrong?"

When he told her the news, she had to take a deep breath. Was she hearing right? "Oh, my God!" Camille exclaimed. She looked into the room at her friend lying in bed and stifled tears. She looked back at Richard, and a single tear escaped his eye.

"Did you tell her mom?" Camille asked him

"No, I couldn't say anything to her, she's already devastated," Richard said.

"Pregnant?"

EPILOGUE

It had been weeks since Camille visited the hospital. The last time she was there, Evelyn had been in a coma and I.V. lines were running about her body. She couldn't begin to imagine what she must be going through or feeling.

"She's awake now," the Doctor had called her a few days ago and said, but she couldn't make it then, she was so consumed with her work and her family. He also said that that she was beginning to talk, but not too much

She thought she had gotten to her in time as she watched Claude deliver that last blow to her skull and cracked it.

My poor Evelyn, she thought as she entered the elevator and pressed the button to the third floor. She thought that she had lost her friend after Claude's brutal attack. Evelyn had been through hell and back, and Camille felt helpless for her friend. She called the hospital the day before, and the nurse said that she was able to breathe on her own and she had even responded a little bit. She wanted to come then, but she was caught up with work and Richard had told her to cover the story with Claude. Camille made sure to have security around the clock at Evelyn's room. She knew that Claude was dead, she had killed him, but she wasn't taking any chances.

As the elevator slowly climbed to the fourth floor, she had an overwhelming feeling that something was wrong. The elevator door finally opened, and Camille made her way to the ICU. When she got to Evelyn's room and stepped over the thresh hold, she realized that the room was empty. The bed had been freshly made. She hurried over to the nurse's station,

"Excuse me, why is that room empty? Did they move the patient that was in there?" Camille asked her.

"What is the patient's name?" the nurse asked.

"Her name is Evelyn, Evelyn Dubois."

The woman punched several keys on the computer then turned to Camille. "Oh yes, Miss Dubois left a couple of hours ago. She was discharged."

"Who discharged her?" Camille asked as her confusion built.

"I don't know, some guy," the nurse said.

Camille took out her cell phone and punched numbers. "Rich, did you know that Evelyn has already been discharged?"

"Tell me you're kidding," Richard said.

"I just got here, and her room is empty, the bed is made, and her things are gone."

"Okay, calm down, Camille. There must be a reasonable explanation for her not being there. When was she due to be discharged anyway?"

"I'm not sure. I'm going to head on over to her house and see if she showed up there."

"Okay, I'll call her mother and see if she is with her, and then I will meet you over there."

Camille left the hospital and sat in her vehicle for a while to think. She knew that Evelyn hated to be in hospitals, so perhaps she had simply discharged herself and gone home. That was the only logical explanation she could think of.

Turning on the car, she headed over to Evelyn's house. On the way, she stopped by a grocery store and bought a bouquet of flowers and a bag of hot beignets. Evelyn loved those; *especially* if they were fresh. Camille was excited about seeing her friend awake and moving around, although she might be in a wheelchair. They could sit and talk, and then she would explain to her why she had lied about being an under-cover agent for the FBI.

Camille wondered if she knew about the pregnancy. She wondered how she handled it when the doctors told her. Whatever the situation was, she was going to be there for her friend.

She had a secret that she had kept all these years. When she found out that Evelyn was pregnant the first time, she knew that Evelyn wanted to get rid of the baby. Evelyn didn't know her at the time, and she adopted Evelyn's baby, only to befriend her years later. She sought her out, she knew she was troubled, but she wasn't sure how she would help her, so she raised Evelyn's baby as her own.

She followed Evelyn many times, from home to work and back home, that was all she did. Then, one night, Evelyn was about to attempt suicide, and she saved her, and they became the best of friends. She tried many times to tell her friend about the baby, but she couldn't for fear that it would ruin the friendship that they had.

An hour later, Camille parked in front of Evelyn's house where she saw Richard sitting in his vehicle like he was talking on the phone. She got out of her car and went to his car and knocked on the window. Richard hung up the phone and stepped out.

"Took you long enough."

"Sorry, I had to run an errand, you didn't go inside?"

"No, I was waiting for you."

"Well, let's go then."

Camille and Richard walked up onto the porch and knocked on the door several times, but there was no answer. They waited then knocked again. The place seemed quiet, and no movement was heard from inside. Camille peaked through the window, but it was barely any light inside.

"Wait. I think she keeps a spare key inside of the flower pot in the back. Wait here," Richard said.

Camille waited patiently then she heard movement in the house.

"Rich? Is everything okay?"

At that moment, Richard opened the front door, and

Camille walked into an empty house. Evelyn was nowhere in sight. Where could she have gone?

"What the hell is going on here, Richard?" Camille asked. "Did she move out?"

"I don't know, I'm going to call her mom now and see if she is with her because something just doesn't feel right," Richard said as he punched his cell phone and stepped outside on the porch. Camille continued to walk through the rest of the house. She checked the kitchen, the cupboards, and everything was still in place. There was no sign that anyone had dirtied dishes or eaten; the fridge was empty except for a half-empty bottle of red wine. Next, she checked the bathroom. Towels on the rack were dry and clean, and the shower was also dry.

Camille heard Richard re-enter the house and came out of the bathroom to meet him. He was standing in the kitchen with one hand on his hip and the other one rubbing his head.

"Anything?" Camille asked.

"Yes, I got her mom. She said Evelyn didn't want to stay in the hospital and she was discharged two days ago. She told her mother that she needed time to rest, and she didn't want to be disturbed. She hasn't heard from her since."

"What are we going to do now, Rich? Evelyn isn't fully recovered yet, and now she's missing. We know Claude didn't take her again because I put a bullet in his head myself. Where could she be? Do you think she may have gone to look for her dad?"

"I don't know, Cam. But we need to find her as soon

as possible before she does something crazy. Did you check every room? Maybe her clothes are still here?"

"I didn't check her bedroom yet."

Richard checked the guest room while Camille checked Evelyn's room. She stopped in the doorway and shouted for Richard.

"Oh, my God! Richard get in here!"

Richard bolted out of the guest room and found Camille standing outside Evelyn's room with her eyes wide and her mouth dropped."

"What's wrong?" he asked, following her gaze to Evelyn's bed.

On the bed in Evelyn's room lay a single black rose with a red ribbon tied around it. And next to it was a white piece of paper folded in half.

Richard walked over and picked up the paper and unfolded it.

R.I.P
Evelyn Rose Dubois

ABOUT THE AUTHOR

Tiffany Forbes is an Architect and Project Manager based in the British Virgin Islands. At a young age, she had a gift for telling stories, and over the years, she began writing short stories for her family and friends to read, while dreaming of one day becoming a published author. She finally got the courage to put pen to paper, and with a burning desire to succeed, she was finally able to write her first of many novels, *The Black Rose*.

 instagram.com/lovably.ty

ACKNOWLEDGMENTS

First and foremost, I thank God for giving me the gifts and abilities to create this story; for without Him, I would not have been able to pursue my dream of writing.

To the memory of my late uncle Cornelius Royal Glasgow, thank you for believing in my dream--even when I didn't.

To my mom, who taught me the value of hard work and staying focused.

To my mentor and coach, Desireé Harris-Bonner, who encouraged, guided, and pushed me when I got stuck on an idea.

For friends and family who said, *"Go for it, girl. You can do it"* when I doubted myself. To all of you I have met over the years, those of whom I have kept in touch with, some of whom inspired the characters for this book... if it weren't for you, I wouldn't be here writing these words.

And, to my readers, for allowing me to fill your minds with the words of my imagination. It took a long time for me to get my thoughts together, and sometimes I wanted to give up and start over, but your prayers and encouragement supported me and kept me going.

Thank you all.

www.ingramcontent.com/pod-product-compliance
Lightning Source LLC
Chambersburg PA
CBHW021029130626
46552CB00005B/1753